Abbot Kinney

Tasks by Twilight

Abbot Kinney

Tasks by Twilight

ISBN/EAN: 9783337250508

Printed in Europe, USA, Canada, Australia, Japan

Cover: Foto ©Andreas Hilbeck / pixelio.de

More available books at **www.hansebooks.com**

BY

ABBOT KINNEY

AUTHOR OF " THE CONQUEST OF DEATH "

G. P. PUTNAM'S SONS

NEW YORK   LONDON
27 WEST TWENTY-THIRD STREET   24 BEDFORD STREET, STRAND

The Knickerbocker Press

1893

Electrotyped, Printed, and Bound by

The Knickerbocker Press, New York

G. P. Putnam's Sons

CONTENTS.

TASKS BY TWILIGHT.

EDUCATION.

" The hard toiler is slow, patient, and conservative, while the student is progressive, as thought will impatiently outrun the slow march
of stubborn reality. By joining study with labor, we combine the
spirit of progress, development, and adaptation with the spirit of conservatism, both so necessary for the historic development of a nation."
—SAMUEL ROYCE.

E DUCATION is generally considered to be the
literary preparation given young persons by teachers at home or in our schools and universities. This is
the commonly received interpretation of the word. It is an
interpretation narrow and incomplete to the last degree.

Education, in its complete sense, is the preparation for
living, and begins at birth. That portion of it obtained
from books and in the schools is the outward flourish,
the trimming and the ornamentation, as compared to
the solid requirements necessary for a successful life.

The absolute essentials for a useful and happy existence are three : First, animal strength—to be a good
animal—to have health, vitality, and physical power.
Without a due amount of this, no other requirements, no
knowledge or information, can be utilized. The physique

must be there to use knowledge. To the extent that physical power or vitality is absent, a human being's knowledge is less useful. As the physique diminishes in power, so must the beneficial activity of the human being be likewise diminished.

The second quality essential to a useful life is the power of observation and adaptation. We must be able to *see* things when we see them ; when we look at a thing we must observe it, recognize its qualities and, remember it. The circumstances in our lives are so varied, so complicated, so changeful, that no rule can be laid down for details in any person's life. Persons do and must depend, in their lives, upon their own individual capacity of observation and adaptation, certainly while any progress takes place in society. We must, if we are successful, act in harmony with the inexorable laws of nature. These laws, never changeable in themselves, are so varied by the circumstances surrounding us, that the rules for successful action in any given person's life must be inscribed and treasured in their own consciousness.

The third quality, without which life must be a failure, is character. By character is meant that combination of qualities which enables us to use the knowledge derived from observation, through our physique, so as to achieve results.

The human animal is gregarious. All human lives are, therefore, affected by the lives of others.

Success may be measured by the capacity an individual has of combining the lives and activities of others, and shaping these to his own ends. For these purposes, a person must have the decision, the perseverance, and the concentration to know what he wants, and to pursue that desire to a conclusion. And above all things he must have the power of securing the confidence and aid of his fellow-men. Energy and honesty are, therefore, important elements in character. Even the chief of a band of thieves must have a degree of honesty to secure the confidence and obedience of his band.

With these three qualities in their perfection, any one reaching maturity will certainly be successful.

The lack of the literary accomplishments and of the useful information furnished by the schools can be and is being every day overcome outside of the schools by those successful without their aid.

The thoughtful will recognize at once that none of these three essentials are customarily· taught in schools. On the contrary, the confined and sedentary life lived by the scholastic student is always detrimental to the physique. Often the consequences result in serious and permanent disability, and not infrequently end in premature death.

The second quality is, as schools are usually managed, equally dwarfed and injured. The thoughts, the statements, and the dogmas of others are taught and memorized at the expense of the individual powers of observation of the student himself. Instead, therefore, of looking at the facts of nature for themselves, and seeing what those facts are, a scholastic person is taught to receive with

little or no question the statements of others in regard
to them. Such influences, therefore, in their purity tend
to prevent a realization of truth and to prevent that personal investigation by which alone we can appreciate its
force.

As to the third requisite the schools are nearly neutral.
They inculcate some of the qualities of character as sort
of side issues. And to this extent they are beneficial.
On the other hand, the system of teaching the dogmas of
others as facts, even when these dogmas are correct,
must have a tendency to diminish the individuality and
self-reliance of the student.

The lack of physical culture, together with the excessive strain on the nervous system, often upsets the balance
of the organism. The reproductive powers suffer especially. An investigation now going on shows, thus far, a
remarkable diminution in childbirth in the literary or
so-called educated classes as compared to the hard
workers.

Upon the whole it is my opinion that, excluding the
playground and taking only the school-room, the results
of an education derived from this source alone would be
of very doubtful advantage.

These words without explanation cast a dark shadow
upon our school system. Such is not my intention.
The value of the thought and experience of others, taught
in our schools, it is impossible to estimate. Our school
systems have been ever increasing in their usefulness and
improving in their methods. The development of late

years has been very great. Owing largely, doubtless, to
the rapidity of its growth, it has not been well balanced.
The literary portion has gone unduly ahead of other
and more essential departments. Qualities developed at
home or on the playground have been neglected through
the increased time required for the literary exercises.
The school has taken more and more the energy of
the child, until now there is scarce any time and practically no energy left for the instruction and experience
derived by young persons from outside sources, and
especially at home. The schools have thus increased
enormously the literary education they originally gave
in small amount, while the absorption of the child's
energy prevents it from learning those things formerly
acquired in the fields, playground, farm, or home.

The school has taken so much of the child's time, that
it now monopolizes the child's educational capacity
without having done anything to give it the class of information it formerly acquired elsewhere. The school
has never taught anything but numbers and letters ; now
that it monopolizes the child, its one-sidedness is a
serious defect. Reforms happily are fast being introduced.

I do not wish to underestimate the great value of the
thought, investigation, and experience of others. We
stand upon the shoulders (as a wise man has said)
of those who have gone before us. We thus have a
broader view, and the smallest of us can see and understands things not appreciated by the giant intellects of the

past. To derive the greatest advantage from the past work of mankind, it is essential to understand the qualities with which nature has endowed us, and the limitations to which we are subject. Parole or book learning is merely the tool which enables us to acquire, with greater facility and rapidity, the knowledge of which we are in search. But it must be clearly understood that it is not the knowledge itself. A man may be a good physician, as far as books are concerned, but until he has worked out and demonstrated the science for himself, until he has had practice and experience, he is not in the true sense a physician. And it is so in everything else. A man may read and be told how to drive a horse, but he is not a horseman until he has worked out the management of the animal by his own experience. The results of the work of others will aid him, and aid him more if he understands that it is not the knowledge itself, but only a tool for the more rapid and facile acquirements of true knowledge.

Books are the guideposts showing the short cuts to knowledge.

The development of individual qualities, individual capacities, and individual character, should always be one of the main aims in education.

Success in life must always depend upon the individual. Self-reliance and the qualities leading to it should be developed. The school, college, and university systems now prevailing among us have no direct influence favoring the real essentials of life, but, as has been pointed out, tend rather to weaken and destroy these qualities.

It is for these reasons, doubtless, that the great men of the Past as well as of the Present have been generally what are called self-made men. It is exceedingly rare that we find any one who has taken the first honors in our schools taking the first place in the contest of life. If this system of schooling were correct, if it really led to a successful life, it must be evident that the greatest success in the school would be followed by the greatest success in life. This is so notoriously not the case that an error must be suspected in our educational system.

Those who graduate from colleges are, for the most part, members of successful and prominent families. They therefore inherit superior qualities and possess superior influence, which with a proper education should push them certainly to the front.

This point indicates their value, it giving to the young the best class of associates. From our associates we derive prejudices and opinions, manners and methods, all of great importance in our life fight.

A system must be judged by its results, and it is generally known that the first-honor men of our colleges are, for the most part, relegated to obscurity on their entry into real life ; thus showing conclusively that success in the school is no passport to success in life.

While our educational system is managed as it is, it would not be well to devote to it the energy or time of the child necessary for graduation with highest honors, because this energy and time can be better used in other directions. But the course now marked out in our schools should not be entirely neglected ; first, because the information there given of the progress of humanity up to our own day is of great importance and advantage, and, second, because it is always well to live understanding one's surroundings and in harmony with them.

Our social system now being so intimately connected with the school, and its standard of what an educated man should be being almost universally received, it would militate against the social standing and happiness of any one not passably familiar with its course.

Another point to consider is the time given to this so-called education or preparation for life. We have now kindergartens, schools, high schools, preparatory schools, colleges, universities, and post-graduate courses. In special avocations, such as law and medicine, it is considered best to pass through all these except the post-graduate course before taking up the specialty. . This requires a great deal of time, often too much time. We certainly ought to consider the length of human life in connection with the length of our theoretical preparation for it. To take all of life for this purpose would be manifestly absurd ; so, also, it would be unwise to take no time for it. The balance to be struck is by that preparation which will enable us to achieve the greatest results.

Correct preparation for life, or, as we say, education, should be a review of the experience of man in his recent evolution, just as the life of the individual from the egg is a review of the evolutionary history of all life.

In this last case we pass through in a few years, days, or hours, what it must have taken our evolutionary progenitors ages to progress beyond. So it must be in education, a general review for all, a special review for the special, and a recognition of the fact that time is of the essence of the contract.

That too much time is often given up to preparation cannot be doubted. Probably a man should commence his life-work between twenty-one and twenty-five, leaning more to the earlier period than to the later. His study may continue till death, but his mere preparation should not longer monopolize his time and activities.

It should be distinctly understood that there is no correct information given in our schools not exceedingly useful and valuable to you, my children.

The point that parents and young persons should consider is that the time of giving this information and the method of giving it, the undue importance given to some lines and the neglect of others, should be avoided and counteracted by you.

In relation to the time of giving information, our schools are much in error. It is the custom now to take very young children,—absorbing most of their time and energy upon a great variety of studies, most of which either have no immediate connection with their surroundings, lives, or future, or no such connection pointed out. The information given is acquired parrot-like—that is to say, it is recited correctly as given in the books, but neither understood in itself nor in its application. A very considerable examination of children, by myself, enables me to say that this statement, while not always, is substantially correct. Reading and study require digestion and assimilation, to be a good food for the mind. Food for the body requires digestion and assimilation, and it may not be considered as stretching matters too far to draw some conclusions from the analogy.

Food is necessary for bodily life and activity. Nothing can be more clear than that the quantity and quality of food that will be useful to us has its characteristics and usefulness qualified and limited by the time and place, and by the activities of our lives.

Climates and occupations govern the quantity and quality of the food that should be taken. Every ounce of food used that is not required is a clog, and besides, necessitates the subtraction of a certain amount of energy from other things to get rid of it.

So, also, the time of life governs the quality and quantity of food that should be eaten. For the infant an exclusive diet of milk is the only appropriate food, for in the infant many of the vital organs are rudimentary. For the grown man stronger and more concentrated foods are requisite. The strong food of the man would kill the baby, the exclusive milk diet of the baby would incapacitate the man. A hungry man requiring food, it is certain, should take only what he needs ; if he were placed in a coop and stuffed like the goose of Strasburg, disease would inevitably ensue. As the liver of the goose becomes by such treatment diseased, so would the liver, and, secondarily, the other organs of the man. Let us now draw the analogy. By the school system of education now prevalent, very young children are cooped up, and, to a great extent, deprived of the natural exercise and experience necessary for the proper development of their qualities of observation and of their physique.

On the other hand, the mental food which all children require, is, in almost all cases, given them in improper quantity and quality. They are literally stuffed like the goose of Strasburg with mental food, not only excessive in quantity, but of that strong and concentrated kind only suited to a mature mind.

As the milk is suited to the baby and the concentrated food to the man, so the simple forms of thought suited to the development of the infant mind should be given the child, and the concentrated form suitable to the man should be given the adult.

The education given our children to-day is as conducive to a mental indigestion as improper food, or excessive quantities of good food, would be to the alimentary digestion.

The same analogy would hold good in other things, as locomotion. The child, first incapable of any locomotion, learns to creep and then to walk. If you undertake to make a baby walk before the natural period has come for this progress, you will, in all likelihood, not only fail, but spoil the youngster's legs into the bargain. So also in sight and touch, the baby sees without seeing, and touches without comprehension. An attempt to drive nature in any of these matters is always dangerous, and generally of doubtful result.

A large amount of the information given at our schools is not understood by the children, and is therefore impossible of application, and is consequently, for the most part, entirely forgotten when they go out into life.

An excessive amount of the child's time is undoubtedly now taken up by our schools.

In England, and especially in Manchester, it has been found that the half-time scholars, who had also to work for their living, surpassed in school attainments those children whose entire time was devoted to study.

This is a clear illustration of the fault. No child should go to school before the age of nine. Four hours is the limit to set for the hours of book study before twelve. No night study should be permitted until after fifteen.

The infant mind before nine, it is true, is capable of a wonderful amount of literary memorizing power, but this apparent knowledge is largely of the same kind as seen in the trick dog, talking parrot, trained horse, etc. The mental powers of the reasoning man are not in the child, consequently no true cultivation of them before they exist is possible.

Children who commence their schooling late, within certain reasonable limits, as a rule, rapidly pass children that have been through previous premature training. It is then apparent that too early schooling not only does no good, but is a positive disadvantage.

If the position of the evolutionist be true, that the young of all animals originate from the egg and pass through previous conditions of life, from the most primitive forms to their present state of development, we can easily perceive the uselessness and impolicy of teaching letters to a suckling baby in a purely animal condition, or philosophy to a child passing through the undeveloped mental condition of the savage.

To the babe, eating, drinking, digestion, and sleep are the lines of usefulness and success ; to the savage largely and to the child entirely, physical development and the observation of nature comprise these conditions. It is only as the human being of the higher development passes out of these steps in a past life, that the supreme attainments of humanity can be understood.

To undertake the teaching of things beyond the stage of development in which the human being affected is at the time is useless in itself, and abstracts force from the evolution of that stage absolutely necessary to be gone through with.

The methods of schooling have improved very greatly, but they have not improved with the same rapidity that the schools have absorbed the time and energy of the children, and have taken these essential elements so that the child's opportunity to obtain the information all animals require by experience is taken away.

The greatest caution that a parent or guardian can exercise, in giving a child an even and well-balanced development, can never be excessive. Not that a parent should take the position of interfering every instant with the child's natural, mental, and physical development, but, on the contrary, these should be given the widest liberty.

What parents should be cautioned against is the undue interference with these natural processes, for the sake of the acquirement of knowledge by the artificial means which are a part of our present system. It must not be overlooked that these artificial processes are of great benefit and aid to the child ; but they should be so carefully guarded as to secure the child against injury of its physique, a thing not very difficult to watch and guard if its importance be appreciated, but also what is far more difficult to recognize, the healthy development of the essential mental qualities of observation, self-reliance, and those other qualities which, taken together, form the individuality and the character of a human being essential to a useful existence.

The kindergarten system has had a great popularity in recent years. Its advantages are great when properly employed, its principles good, and its drawbacks considerable. This is, indeed, an unsatisfactory ending for a system that has been received with so much hope by the lovers of mankind. It is now pretty clear that the kindergarten is but a poor substitute for the home nursery, and is most useful to the children of the poor, whose mothers work out or are dead, or otherwise incapable of caring for them.

The very young child is better and stronger, mentally as well as physically, in the country, roaming and playing wild and unkempt, than in the best kindergarten ever established ; but older ones may be much benefited by it.

It is probable that no school system can ever take the .place of nature as a teacher. In the early years of life little book information that is ever used is obtained. Compared to the time devoted by children to schooling, the information assimilated is almost nothing. The healthy child, mentally and physically well balanced, will learn more in one year at the age of fifteen of the common-school education, and understand its applications better, than in the ten years before this time. While this is generally known to be true of most children, the question arises as to how much a previous course of training may assist the acquisition of knowledge at the really receptive period of the child for book information.

The close confinement of the school-room, the sedentary life, and the absorption of the energies from other lines of development must be injurious. Children vary greatly in the times and quality of their development, and it is for the parent to watch this in each child carefully, and suit the class of information given to the unfolding powers. Taking everything into consideration, it would seem wiser to err on the side of sending the child to school too late rather than too early.

The early and continuous school attendance of children undermines and weakens the home influence and the family tie. The parents rely more and more on the school for complete instruction and education, and more and more neglect home and family influence. The schools are without religion, and there seems no way to introduce it in any form. The absorption by them of time and energy, and the reverence in which the system is largely held, as a matter of fact exclude any living religious force from the lives of the great majority of school children. As a consequence we are drifting faster than we know into a nation without a religion.

Habits of application and industry should by all means be imparted to a child. The natural curiosity and desire for knowledge is great in every child. Let these qualities be improved and rewarded.

Nothing is perhaps so generally overlooked as the fact that a child appreciates reward in return for its labor as much as, if not more than, a grown person. Their sense of injustice is keen, their appreciation of the family relation and the labor of the parent to give them a living, imperfect ; that is, they take for granted the living that the parent gives them, and seldom feel perfectly satisfied in performing labor, whether mental or physical, not directly rewarded in them as it is in others.

Parents who desire to see their children industrious, mentally or physically, should not disguise from themselves this fact. A motive for work and labor should always be given.

Habits of industry can almost always be imparted to children if they receive a compensation which they can understand. In imparting mental information, a clear and proximate reason for its acquisition should be given, utilizing as far as practicable the natural curiosity of the child. Build from one thing to another, show relationships and connections, bearing ever in mind the condition and limitations of the child's brain.

Education in the broadest view commences at birth and only ends with death. Consciously or unconsciously we are always receiving impressions which are information ; these may be applied or unapplied,—they may be used for good or for evil. The schooling or the ordinary processes to which the word education is commonly applied is, as has been said, merely the tool for a more facile appreciation of facts and their proper application, as these come to us through our experience. The truth must never be lost sight of that the only real knowledge is obtained by experience—the only application of knowledge comes through practice.

Work and labor is the price we must pay for everything we do well. Mere parrot-like repetition of the experience of others is not knowledge. The school-boy acquires proficiency in his games only by attention, application, and labor.

A successful player of games is devoting as much time and energy to the game in which he succeeds, as the mechanic or book student to his line of work. Only by thought and effort can success be accomplished.

2

Life is labor. From the gambler at his cards and the young man at his tennis, to the successful farmer, merchant, or statesman, all derive what proficiency they may have by experience, attention, and hard work.

The thing to do with a young person is to direct the energies into those channels which will produce good and useful results, and to teach them that the hardest work, and the most unremunerative devotion of energy, is always given to a dissolute life and occupation inimical to the interests of themselves and of society,— inimical to their own interests because such occupations are invariably wearing upon the constitution and vitality, dwarfing to the better qualities of the mind, destructive to the physique, and condemned by one's fellow-men.

A proper understanding by a young person of the true object of life, of the reasonableness of the general rules of society, the foundation of its prejudices in the accumulated experiences of mankind, and the relation of effort to result, ought, if properly inculcated, to prevent any normally constituted child from devoting its energies to useless or injurious effort.

Some of the points elucidating this position will be presented in other chapters. In this will be given only an outline of what seems to be the proper course to pursue as to the three great essentials already named, and to the book-learning beneficial as an aid in acquiring them, and in giving the agreeable polish and finish to the life of a thorough-bred.

PHYSIQUE.

A sound body gives a sound mind. The physique is the first thing to be considered in a child after it is born, and it is a thing absolutely necessary to maintain in a good condition throughout life.

Irritable tempers, visionary ideas, immoral thoughts and acts are largely the result of diseased or of imperfectly developed bodies. Those whose physical health is sound are usually sound in their minds and morals.

A person to be healthy must have a well-developed physique,—each organ performing its proper function.

To secure this result the muscles must be exercised. Without physical exercise, which is labor, the vital organs will not properly perform their duties. Exercise may be of two kinds. One is that which is devoted to recreation, as in games, hunting, or athletic sports, etc. ; the other, that which is devoted to directly remunerative employments, such as agricultural work, or that in any of the mechanical or useful occupations. Both of these are beneficial as well to the body as to the mind. Those who do not have sufficient bodily exercise in one of these two ways, lose in the tone and quality not only of their bodies but of their minds also.

Indigestion, the most prompt and easily recognized result of lack of physical exercise, is always accompanied by a greater or less degree of discomfort and unhappiness, and acts unfavorably, as well on those who are its victims, as upon those who come in contact with them.

Thus the great happiness naturally the outcome of family life is diminished, and sometimes altogether un-done. Good digestion, good health—these are essentials in happiness.

Look through your acquaintances and remark how often the starting-point of quarrels, misunderstandings, nagging, irritation, and unkind feelings arises from imper-fect digestion, imperfect bodily development, or a bodily disease coming from a lack of the proper use of the physical powers.

The physique is the first thing to be considered. It is the first thing that we can consider in the child when born. When properly developed, it leads to a healthy mental and moral condition, and enables its happy pos-sessor to use with the greatest benefit any mental acquirements.

Before the age of sixteen, at least one-half of the day should be devoted to out-door exercises. The treatment of boys and girls in regard to physical development must, from the limitations placed by nature on the female sex, be entirely different.

BOYS.

The exercise given by games is a thing boys should never be deprived of. The amusement, interest, and emulation produced by games lead to voluntary use of the muscles. Games where only one or two are engaged upon a side, or in which no combination is required, such as bowling, tennis, fencing, boxing, etc., are very good. Tennis is perhaps of all games the one which gives the most complete exercise to all the muscles, with the least strain, of any that we have. But one of its great advantages, that is, that it requires only two to play the game, is also a great drawback to it as an educator. Games requiring combination, discipline, and unity of action demonstrate in a reasonable way to a child the great value of these in life.

The discipline that is so often only produced in the schoolroom, and, unfortunately, only too often in the family by the fiat of the master or the parent, is secured in such games as base-ball, foot-ball, cricket, etc., by its evident utility for a successful issue. Thus, we often see the boy who in the school-room is a revolutionist or a rebel, the most prompt in obeying the orders of his captain in a game, in carrying out his own duties in that game, and maintaining discipline amongst the others engaged in it.

It must be evident that the frequent difficulty school-masters find in maintaining the discipline in their school-rooms, as compared with the facility with which the game captains maintain the discipline of their games, with the same boys, is worthy of attention.

The discipline of a game offers a lesson most valuable for the boy to learn. It requires him to develop his individuality in harmony with his surroundings, to govern his temper, and to specialize his energies in common with those of others to achieve a well-defined end. These qualities are exceedingly valuable in after life, far more so than we commonly realize.

The development of character, of self-discipline, and of organization given by well-ordered games, together with the physical development, the health and the constitution, which they give or maintain, is more valuable than all the other results produced in the school put together.

The playground is now one of the first things sacrificed in our ever-increasing population and the consequent increased value of land. There are probably not a dozen schools of the thousands situated in our cities and towns that have an adequate playground. The denser the population and the less outside opportunity for play and its organization, discipline, and exercise, the more certain are we to find the playground too small or absent.

Parents should give more than usual attention to secure to their boys the benefits of these games, and thus counteract the tendencies of the times. By all means have your boys play games. I have observed in the French schools, where games requiring combination are seldom played, a distinct physical and moral deterioration in the boys.

The energy of the boy, which under the Anglo-Saxon system of having these games goes so largely to promote his physical welfare and to promote those other useful qualities spoken of, goes in the French boy to an abnormal and precocious development of the sexual instinct.

These instincts, so grand, so magnificent, and so God-

like in their proper use, making of us creators, giving
sound health and giving a happiness which can be in no
other way attained, in their abuse destroy the physique,
weaken the mind, undermine morality, and promote that
greatest curse that can befall a family—sterility and
extinction.

Of the exercises requiring no combination of persons,
boxing is perhaps one of the best. In this the physical
powers are generally used, and in young persons with
small danger of strain, while at the same time the temper
is well disciplined (for in boxing a display of temper is a
weakness) and the animal courage must be developed.
One of its disadvantages is that its ethics demand that
only one kind of blows should be struck, whereas in
real physical contests, such as might occur in being attacked by a footpad, all blows leading to conquest should
be used without any reference to whether they are fair
or foul.

With the trained boxer, boxing ethics will be an instinct
and he will be unable to strike any but the regulation
blows.

Many persons think boxing brutal ; in practice, however, it has proved a safe outlet for the passions and
rivalries common with all healthy boys. For the human
being, it must be remembered, commences in the infant
with the purely animal instincts of eating, digestion, and
sleep, and goes on from the purely animal through the
lower stages of human society—as shown in the savage
and barbarian—up to the fully developed civilized man.

The egg from which all life comes is the commencement of the human being. All life commencing with this
goes through the stages of previous development. Many
of these stages in the human being are gone through in
the fœtus : such as the rudimentary gills which the fœtus
at one time has, then a condition similar to the lower
mammalia, then a hairy one similar to the monkey, and
so on to birth, and afterward till the age of 25 or 30, when
the highest qualities of civilized man are or ought to be
perfected. The savage stage is a clearly defined one in
every boy's life and should be recognized and provided for.

Boxing gives a safe outlet which, amongst the Latin
races and other peoples not having it or a safe substitute,
is taken by the knife, the pistol, or other deadly weapons.
The effects of the use of the hands instead of the use of
deadly weapons for satisfying the personal contests that
occur universally amongst boys, are shown in the after
history of these as men.

Boys and formed communities brought up in the
Anglo-Saxon method are seldom found carrying deadly
weapons, and still more seldom found using them ; whereas amongst the Latin races, which have no such system,
the knife is commonly carried and very frequently used.
And besides, the practice of openly facing an enemy not
having been inculcated, these people with no natural defects of courage generally use their deadly weapons from
an ambush and stab in the back. Thus courage is cultivated in the Anglo-Saxon and dwarfed in the Latin race ;
the result being that, man for man, in all the numerous

contests these races have had either between each other or with nature, the Anglo-Saxon has proved the best fighter and the best pioneer. It is a pity that our American boys in cities are so often brought up in the Latin system.

Scarcely too much can be said to inculcate the value of games, not alone from a physical point of view but especially as tending to the strengthening of the morals. No games or physical exercises can be well carried on by those who are the victims of vice. Over-eating, improper diet, indulgence in narcotics or stimulants, abuse of the reproductive organs, any and all, immediately show themselves in reduced physical capacity. The successful athlete must be a virtuous man and lead a well-ordered life. Thus the need of morality is seen as a means of success.

The system of recording athletic performances, of timing one's self in races, in measuring jumps, the putting of the shot, the number of times the bull's-eye is hit by rifle shooters, etc., all force upon the attention of the practising contestant the injurious result of any excess, of any abuse of the body, or of any mistake in living.

The prize-fighter who uses alcohol must, when he is about to undertake a contest, reform and eschew it altogether for a considerable time and go into what is called training. The hours of sleep are plentiful, the exercise continuous, the diet plain and easily assimilated. The body is cared for, the nerves are cared for, and so is morality cared for in more ways than one.

It is very important to show children the value of training in their sports. By training is meant practice, hard work, and attention to all things that affect the body, such as diet, sleep, cleanliness, health, and a virtuous life.

When the boy sees the beneficial effect of these, in beating his competitors in the sports in which he may be interested, it will be well to point out with forcibleness that the same attention to these matters, directed to his pursuits in later life, will prove alike successful and enable him to triumph over those naturally his superiors.

Galton, one of the best English investigators and philosophers of our time, says that the population of the Greek cities during their palmy days had a much higher intellectual average than that of any civilized people now.

The artistic, architectural, and intellectual works that this comparatively small population left show that they must have had indeed a very high development.

When we examine their institutions, we find that their education was all done out-of-doors.

The word academy, which we have taken from the Greek to mean an educational institution, signifies a grove, and has come to have its other meaning, because the Greek philosophers taught in groves. Their education, too, was little, if at all, in the line of parrot-like memorizing ; for the old philosophers acted more as guides in developing the intellects and reasoning powers of their disciples.

We find, also, that the athletic sports had an immense

development in Greece. The names of many of the champions of the Olympian games are familiar to us to this day. The importance attached to physical exercise was great in Greece, and the young men exercised more or less in the national games. Hand and hand with the physical development went the intellectual. The Greek statues that we have show the physical perfection to which that race must have arrived when these were made.

The works of Homer, Plato, Socrates, Euclid, Aristotle, and many others indicate their intellectual development. The history of the Greek people shows beyond any controversy that physical development is no bar to that of intellect. On the contrary, there is every reason to think that the physical and vital power of the race, created by athletic sports, was a prominent cause of its intellectual achievements. The rock on which the Greek people split was doubtless the weakening of the family tie and the non-reproduction of the superior class, owing to the accumulated wealth and the lack of impressing the importance of reproduction on the young people.

It takes a very short time for a family or a race to disappear from the world, when they do not reproduce themselves. The Roman Conquest accentuated these causes, and the old Greek intellectual race has disappeared from the face of the earth, and left no trace in a living people behind it.

But this should not prevent us from taking advantage of what was good in their civilization, while avoiding that which was bad. The Greek civilization teaches us the great benefit of bodily exercise in perfecting physical and intellectual beauty.

Have your boys play games and take an interest in all athletic sports. Another advantage which can be taught them by this means is that of devoting their energies and attention to one particular game or exercise.

The value of concentration is as great in these physical exercises as it is in anything in after life, and this fact should be taught. No exercise should be encouraged, however, which does not develop the body evenly. Such exercises therefore as bowling, bicycling, etc., which develop only portions of the body, often at the expense of others, are inferior.

The individual taste of a boy should, with these exceptions, be given full play. There is one exercise, however, that all boys should be taught, and that is swimming. There are so many occasions when a boy's life may be saved by this art, that it should by no means be neglected.

Horseback exercise should also be taught whenever the parents' means permit. For this exercise develops courage, the faculties of command, and the necessity of a good condition of the animal used. To develop this latter point, the boy should take care of his own horse, for at least a certain time, until he is thoroughly familiar with what ought to be done to keep it in good condition.

MANUAL LABOR.

While games and athletic sports should never be neglected and should even be encouraged into mature life, physical labor of a different kind is equally important.

At a very early age children should be given an opportunity of earning money by the labor of their hands. Work about the garden, in the orchard, or on the farm, or in any out-door pursuit that may be convenient, will prove of the greatest advantage.

Without the reward it will be seldom found that a young person will take much interest in manual labor. On the contrary, some little remuneration will lead them to acquire the useful habit of bending their efforts to result. One of the best means of doing this is to set aside for them a little garden patch and pay them for the products ; or a few chickens, paying for the eggs or poultry ; a pig or two, or, if there be sufficient cattle on the farm, give them a cow or two and allow them to manage the breeding as well as the general care of the animals.

For the girls, poultry, pigeons, or a plot of roses and flowers, paying for the eggs, the roses, or flowers, is a good method.

In some such way as this, the child will cultivate habits of industry, thought, self-reliance, and independence, and these should be handed down from father to son and from generation to generation.

Recompense your children for their labor, as far as is possible ; for the work they do and the result they achieve. If you pay a boy by the day for killing rats or gophers, for gardening, or for attention to the farm, or pay him for the number of rats or gophers he kills, the milk he gets from his cows, the eggs from his chickens, the fruit from his orchard, or the vegetables from his garden, the difference in result will be great and astonishing. The difference in the material results achieved is but a faint indication of the difference of results upon the character of your child. Habits of industry and the practical business view of life-effort which he acquires is incalculably greater than by any mere machine or routine drudgery.

What is drudgery in one case is an occupation—nay, a pastime in the other. With all of this the out-door work maintains and develops the physique, the vitality, and the morality of the child.

Boys should be given at first, as far as possible, familiarity with an out-door occupation. The circumstances and location of the family and the natural bent of the child should be given due consideration in selecting the occupation to be taught.

The child should in every case commence at the bottom or alphabet of the occupation, with the distinct object ever held in view of obtaining a scientific and skilful grasp of the whole, and of attaining by capacity and work its highest rewards.

There is no labor or effort in the world but what will make a man reputed and even great when thoroughly, skilfully, and well done. Even the slightest, most menial, or most primitive work attached to any occupation may be so well done as to give honor both to the work itself and to the worker.

The occupation which more than any other seems to have resulted in developing the individuality and greatness of a country is agriculture. The ultimate and continual contact with the grandest operations of nature, given by agriculture, may be well understood as having produced this result.

The agriculturist is a continual witness of the evolution of nature. He sees the most brilliant flowers blossom from the fetid manure. From death springs life. The great processes of germination, of birth of plants and animals, are continually before him. The value of proper seeds and proper breeds is continually a guide to the proper employment of his own reproductive powers. The laws of nature directly correct his errors of judgment or practice. Ever with nature, he is ever with truth, and from truth comes greatness. It is probably from these causes that not only the ranks of the great but the whole population of the world are ever recruited from the agricultural classes.

If the beauty and wonders of natural processes be pointed out, as occurring on the farm, to the boy, and his labor be fairly remunerated, and the work called for be not excessive, there is no occupation, in my opinion, at once so attractive and instructive, so beneficial alike to the physique, the mind, and character, as that of agriculture.

It is essential that a child should not be allowed to work excessive hours, much less forced to do so. An excess of drudgery is injurious to both body and mind,

and kills originality. A due balance in this regard should
be carefully struck, and it should be remembered in
doing this that children's capacities and endurance vary
as much as their faces.

After farming, carpentering is perhaps the best occupation to teach. The uses of a carpenter's work are mani-
fold. It is a trade which can be taught or practised
almost anywhere. It is an occupation full of variety, full
of development, and therefore full of interest. A vast
amount of carpenter work can be done alone. Thus
originality and self-reliance are developed. The trade
also calls for combination in many of its lines of activity,
which gives the idea of the value of organization in effort.

Labor may be so formal and perfunctory as to counter
progress. Labor drudged off into a mechanical routine
tends to assimilate the faculties used to instinct. The
worker under such circumstances goes on not only without thought or improvement, but may actually degenerate.
Thus some kinds of work are only good to understand or
to have practice in, but are not good for regular employment. All work full of regular repetition is eventually
dwarfing.

The dignity of labor—the fact that human beings cannot be healthy or happy without using their faculties—
which means work, either unproductive as in games, or
productive in the ordinary sense of labor, should be
continuously impressed on children from their earliest
receptive period.

To secure an appreciation and liking for work, it is

absolutely essential to give the person working a fair proportion of the returns of his labor.

People can be made to work without this, but can never be made to understand the dignity and the necessity of labor without it. Health and happiness are inextricably interwoven with and have their life in occupation. The development of our physique and of our minds can only come by using them. The non-use of our muscles or our faculties will surely result in diminished power. If a man break his arm, it is placed in a sling till the bone knit again ; meantime the muscles remain unused ; these commence and continue to atrophy and wither and weaken while unused ; if the non-use be kept up too long the original power will never return. It has not been clearly demonstrated that a similar result comes from the non-use of our intellectual qualities, but my own personal experience has proved to me that a similar cause will produce a similar effect as well in the brain as in the body, and I have found in practice that the leaving in idleness of any faculty is at once followed by rust and an incapacity to its former full use.

PRACTICE MAKES PERFECT.

This position can be impressed on children by showing them that in their every-day occupations practice leads to the strengthening and better use of their faculties in any given direction, makes the labor even in a game more easy and automatic, and tends to perfection ; while lack of practice and lack of use of the faculties increases the

3

elements of uncertainty and error, weakens the powers, increases labor, and diminishes results. These matters can be easily taught through the games and occupations of childhood, and should be repeatedly applied again and again to the independent and self-reliant life to which the child is eventually destined.

Idleness breeds laziness. While this depletes the body and mind force, it has only a too well recognized tendency to cause an abnormal and premature development of the sexual instincts. In those too young to satisfy those grand aspirations legitimately, it is almost certain to produce license, profligacy, crime, and eventually a destruction of the healthy and proper enjoyment and exercise of these grand and necessary functions. Outdoor exercise, out-door life, healthy labor, and contact with nature are by all means the best safeguard and corrective against this greatest misfortune which can befall an individual, a family, or a race.

By the proper development of a physique, of habits of industry and of observation, character will come of itself. But it is well for the parent to continually cultivate in a child an appreciation of the grandeur of truth, of which faithfulness, honesty, and the performance of duty are but offshoots.

Direct punishment of a child is scarcely ever a good thing. But a child to learn must be punished for error. That punishment should be made, as far as possible, to come from themselves. When they hurt themselves by falling, by injudicious acts, or by carelessness, point out to them that their hurt, mental or physical, comes from their own act, comes from violating the inexorable laws of nature. The consequences of such violation will be visited on them more and more as they become older, more independent, and necessarily more reliant on their own efforts.

If these lessons be not understood or be injudiciously avoided, they will surely come in later life accompanied by more serious injuries than they are when learned young, by bumps, scratches, wounded feelings, etc., for minor offences against the laws of nature.

The laws of man written in reason or unwritten, and founded in prejudice and instinct, are only good as long as they are in harmony with nature. But all of these should be obeyed and followed, unless, after careful examination, conscientious thought, and study and due deliberation, they are found to be not in harmony with progressive nature.

It must be remembered that the history of mankind is one of ups and downs, of liberty and restraint, swinging now to one extreme and now to another, but always in the main the efforts of man have been directed consciously and more often unconsciously to harmonize his race development with nature. Where he has missed his aim he has erred, and if his regulations depart too far from natural law the result is the destruction of that line of progress, almost always followed by the destruction of that part of the race that originated and practised such error. So have disappeared Tyrians, Egyptians, Carthaginians, Greeks, Romans, and innumerable nations and peoples.

A character founded on untruth or error is of necessity inferior, and would be desired by no one. Therefore, truth alone should be taught. Truth elevates the character. A devotion to it leads to an insight into nature, which is true, and this leads to lasting success and to greatness. Error must fail; truth must triumph. The result is inevitable; it is written in the experience of mankind. Men and even generations of men have at times struggled painfully with error, only to fail and disappear in the end.

Seek out truth, hold fast to it, teach it to your children. Never allow some apparent advantage to tempt you from the path and thus to take the first step in the downward course to destruction. Truth and justice are eternal; as you wish to be eternal, to see your children and your children's children eternal, be steadfast in truth.

He who lives by truth must be in the right. In the whole experience of mankind there has never been any other position permanently successful. It must be remembered that temporary or even permanent success for one's self is a comparatively small achievement without success for one's children and descendants. Man in himself lives but a span; he lives but to die. In his children, however, his vital spark, his qualities, his likeness, his life, go on from generation to generation, and the presumption is reasonable that through a perfected race he will reach eternity. To achieve this grand destiny, he must form his life and progress in harmony with nature's laws. In no way can this be done by falsehood. Truth alone is the guide to eternal life. There is no weapon of offence in life's strength, no armor of defence, that can compare to truth. Comprehend the truth, follow it in all things, and be in the right.

He so armed and so defended is thrice armed, thrice fortified.

Police executing the laws of society often take men much their superior physically, to judgment. Sometimes single-handed seize them from a crowd of sympathizers. As laws are true and just, as they harmonize with the verity of nature and the real interests of society, so does this power of police increase. On the other hand, laws departing from right, and to the extent that these so depart from justice, their execution by the police is weakened, and when reduced to physical force alone is paralyzed.

The consciousness of right gives confidence. It gives a nerve or moral force that enables to a fuller use of physical or mental powers than any sophistry or error can give.

Error is weakness. Its victim's force is always sapped. Error takes from strength, never gives it. As the saying goes : " Error walks abroad disguised ; were she to appear unmasked, she would be mobbed in the streets."

Tear down the disguise from yourself and your children. Temporary advantages, respite from judgment, an immediate money gain, may sometimes appear to be available through some lie, deception, or travesty of the truth. Such cases are but for the moment. They are gained, if gained at all, at a permanent sacrifice of character, self-respect, and of actual force.

As self-respect is lost, so is lost the power of commanding the respect of others. Honesty is undoubtedly the best policy for all life success. It develops and strengthens our best powers. It attracts and maintains the confidence of those around us.

A lie is hard to kill. It continually comes back to plague us. Nearly all deception leads to further deception. One lie breeds another. To get out of one awkward situation by falsehood is to create many other situations which in the end demand the truth. A lie means uneasiness, much work, much trouble, and, as a rule, the truth must be brought in to make things go right in the end. Thus the labor and pain of lying are naught.

The most important reason for avoiding untruth is the inevitable weakening and injury to the character of him who lies. It is not alone the respect and confidence of those around you that is involved, but your own proper respect and confidence in yourself. A liar throws away the keystone of all success—self-confidence.

Be most careful in this. Teach truth. Give your children a devotion to it, a confidence in it, that will never be shaken. For this purpose you will find no school like nature.

Truth is like the polar star, ever steadfast, ever bright,

ever faithful ; hidden sometimes by the gross vapors of the earth, we need but a little patience and our guiding star will again appear. We always know where to look for it.

A man who is known to always work conscientiously, to be right, whose word is as good as his bond, will, beyond any peradventure, obtain a hold upon his fellow-men that nothing else will give. Intrigue and trading may temporarily obscure him, as the clouds do the north star ; turmoil and the pettiness of society may draw away the attention of the people from such a man, but when danger comes, when a crisis is at hand, his opponents will disappear like mist before the sun, and his head will rise above his fellows as surely as the sun rises in the morning to dispel the mists of night.

Whether you be of ordinary or great ability, be honest, be true, be in the right, and your achievements will be grander and your fame more permanent than by any shystering, intriguing, or pettiness that was or ever will be invented.

You cannot be great in anything unless you act in harmony with its verities. Any departure from truth will weaken your character and diminish your capacity to perceive the truth in your chosen pursuit, and if the departure be considerable, you will be damned to be an incompetent trickster.

The truth has no connection with coarseness or brutality. Some individuals, even some nations, confuse the two, and thus lose the taste for truth. In the ordinary affairs and social intercourse of life, tact and politeness are of very great value. There is always something pleasant to be done at very slight cost. There is always something pleasant to be said that is true. The amenities of life add much to its attractiveness. A person with tact will secure support and arrive at results that one of superior ability without it could not attain.

Flattery is praise not founded on truth, or commendation not meant, and is a deception intended to obtain results from the vanity of the flattered. It weakens both giver and receiver, and should never be practised. Tact and politeness come from the heart and are the mirror of true sympathy and feeling.

The forms of politeness, such as good-day, good-night, shaking hands, visiting, and the etiquette of social intercourse, are the results of the experience of mankind as to the best means of expressing kind feeling. Good manners indicate the thoroughbred. Good manners are a great aid to success; they are essential, and should be taught. In teaching them, never cease to impress upon the young person the fact that good manners are founded on good feeling. The hollow forms of etiquette may be gone through with correctly and still leave the recipient ill at ease or unhappy. This is not good manners. On the other hand, one may have a heart full of sympathy and kindness and still be so unable to express it, or so ignorant of what to do or when to do it, that such a one is looked upon as cold or rude.

Good feeling may exist without good manners. Good

manners cannot exist without good feeling. There is in every normal human being a fund of good feeling ; cultivate this in your children, and teach them what man's experience has found to be the best means of giving it expression and of thus pleasing those around us. In social intercourse the truth is just as essential as it is anywhere else. No little falsehoods should be practised in human intercourse. ·You should not say you are out when you are in. There are, however, a great many truths that, if uttered, would not conduce to good feeling. Silence in such matters should be the rule. Never speak of an unpleasant matter unless you have a clearly thought out object in view. In society speak of pleasant truths ; leave unpleasant ones alone.

There is one rule in human intercourse which should be impressed on young people from the commencement, and that is always to accentuate and bring into prominence things upon which you and those around you agree, and always keep those things upon which you do not agree out of conversation, and only to be brought to view in some short and extreme moment when action is deciding whether a thing shall be as they wish it or as you wish it. Stick close to your main points, but be liberal in details and non-essentials.

When you oppose, cultivate silence and action. When you agree, study combination, keep your attention to the main point and object to be secured. Avoid controversies on unimportant details, and avoid all controversies, as far as possible, with those who act with you.

Take advantage of opportunities when they come, and make them when they do not.

Young people will not be able to be perfect in anything at once. Competency in all things comes slowly. The child learns to walk only after effort and repeated failure. Failure at first must be expected and taken for granted. Do not blame a child for what is inevitable. Study continually how to guide them to avoid error. Show them where they have gone wrong and the causes of their failure. Do not even lead a child to think mistake and failure a disgrace. On the contrary, tell them that this is to be expected. Not to succeed eventually is disgrace, but many mistakes are to be expected, nay, in humanity are inevitable on the way. These mistakes which all persons do and must make in life are useful as teachers or as so many guideposts on bad roads or no thoroughfares to warn us not to take them again.

Life has often been compared to a journey. It is a journey through a country sometimes confusing us with a maze of roads, some bad, some good, some going nowhere, some going backward, and others in advance, some going round about, some going direct. In other places we have a trackless country into which, if we venture, we must trust entirely to our bearings being correct for a happy exit.

The foundation principles and great and immutable truths, if understood and followed, will not perhaps prevent all deviations from the most direct path to permanent success and to immortality, but they will, beyond peradventure, prevent serious and fatal departures from that path, and will furnish a sure guide to a speedy return to it when we do miss our way.

Individuals and races have, when successful, followed the direct road. Thus far in life no nation has gone ahead of the world and remained ahead. History is a chronicle of the rapid rise and rapid decay of peoples. The reason of their advance was that they were right, that they were on the true, direct road. The reason of their decay has been that they left the true road, did wrong, and wasted their strength and time in no thoroughfares.

Encourage children to persistence. Teach them to conquer the impediments and overcome the obstacles which do and always will exist in any life effort. Be careful to show children that obstacles exist everywhere and in every line of effort. The art of life is to have the persistence to overcome them, or get around them when they are too large or too difficult.

Of the two qualities—persistence in attack upon obstacles, and the strategy to circumvent them—persistence is by far the most valuable. Obstacles always appear in every walk of life and in everything we attempt to accomplish. Things often appear difficult, even impossible of accomplishment, that can be and are achieved by perseverance.

At the same time, there is such a thing as wasting time and energy on the extremely difficult or impossible. To draw the line between these two must be a matter for the judgment of the individual. The benefit of the doubt, however, must always be given to perseverance.

If you can thoroughly impress upon children the idea that they should go into nothing that they do not intend to come out of victorious, that they must expect obstacles and calculate on making mistakes before the great object is achieved, and induce a habit of looking over the ground of any result they wish to attain and taking account of the difficulties that lie in the path of all things, from a childhood game to the most serious work of life, you will have done much to secure their future success.

It should always be an effort of a parent or a teacher to secure the confidence of the child and to make companions of them. The standard set should indeed be a high one, but it is of the greatest importance to realize that the standard can only be achieved through a progressive development ; that neither character nor success can be picked up ready-made ; that these must be worked out and developed in the individual, and that this result can only come through the lessons given us by overcoming obstacles. Failures and lack of success at first are not a disgrace, but are to be expected and conquered.

The higher the standard set, the more necessary is it to follow this rule. To set an exceedingly high standard, and then to teach children that every failure in their attempt to reach it is a disgrace, must result in discouraging the child and driving it to despair. This point has been somewhat enlarged on in the chapter on the Treatment of the Child.

Many life failures are owing entirely to this error. This rule should apply not only to the direct and material interests of life, but also to the moral qualities. We must remember that a child's moral nature is quite as much a matter of growth and development as the physical or mental. The one may be maimed, distorted, weakened, or diseased, as well as the other.

The body has no monopoly of sickness. The mental health may be undermined as well as the physical. The one depends very largely on the other, but the most disastrous sickness is that of the mind. Strengthen the body and you strengthen the mind and moral qualities. Strengthen the mind and the moral qualities and you strengthen the body.

The aim of the educator should, therefore, be to maintain a reasonable balance between the three.

The physical results achievable by the man are impossible to the child ; still, the standard should be that attainable by the man, recognizing, however, that that standard can only be obtained after years of growth and effort. Never call upon the child for the impossible.

So also in what to many is far less evident, that is that the moral and mental qualities also grow and develop. The standard set should be the highest ; but that standard can never be attained by the child. A human being, while a child, is going through a state of evolution. It is growing and developing in its mental and moral qualities just as much as it is in its physical.

The teacher should never unduly blame a child for the imperfect acts or thoughts, the evidence of a transition state ; for such a course can only result in the discouragement of the child.

A properly brought up child will feel, if it does not perceive through the reason, that its imperfect physical or mental traits are a part of its nature.   The non-recognition of this fact, and the undue blame or punishment of outcroppings of nature, can never strengthen the child or lead it to cure these defects, but must, on the contrary, produce an opposite result.   The greatest departures from true mental balance, as from moral conduct, is by those of diseased bodies or by those living an unnatural life.

The limited receptive capacity of children for the highest thoughts and the highest education is a double reason for never sacrificing the physique in the early periods of life, to teach things which are really learned only by rote and not understood.   .

Up to and safely beyond the age of puberty, the first thought of the parent and of the educator should be the physique.   The best as well as the most impressive and lasting education is that of object teaching and personal experience.   This can be and should be mainly taught outdoors.   Put the child's hand in that of Nature and the progress made must be true.

Such a system of education for the mind and faculties, it is almost impossible to conceive of as going on without a corresponding education and development of the physique.

The difficulty of educating large numbers of children in this way, and the probability, therefore, that such a system will never be in general use by the community, should not dull the parent's appreciation of its value, but should lead him to redoubled effort to secure to his children the correct system which there must always be so great a tendency to suppress.

The objection to such a system is, that it may be so conducted as to neglect the mental training necessary to concentrate the faculties upon a definite purpose, and to acquire technical information necessary for the highest achievement.

In the medical schools it is said that those students, who have previously graduated at some university, acquire their medical education more easily and stand higher in their classes than those students who have not been university men. Whether the advantage continues in the outside contest, I have not had an opportunity of investigating.

This fact shows that mental training, as given in the schools, has some advantages. Of course the question at once arises as to the comparative value of the four year university course and four years of medical college study, or the eight years of medical work to the intending physician. It is contended that the liberal education, as it is called, of the university, will help the medical student more than the entire period devoted to medicine. It seems, however, that seven or eight years' medical study and hospital work, with some reasonable devotion to general reading, would make a more accomplished physician than four years of university work and three or four of medicine.

With this possible weakness in view, a special attention should be given to practise the mind of the young person to acquire dry and perhaps tiresome details, so as to have this power in later life. Such detail study should always be so directed as to conduct the student to the comprehension of some familiar object.

Many men, placed in prominent positions by birth or accident, have failed to properly manage their own or other people's affairs, while remarkably skilled in details connected with these.

A number of the failures amongst the Roman emperors were phenomenally skilled in the details of military exercise. Our own General McClellan was an instance of this : acquainted with every detail of war and its management, he accomplished nothing decisive with the great army at his command.

Louis XVI. was a locksmith of merit, but no statesman ; and so the instances might be multiplied. The Chinese have written examinations to pass for political position. To pass these a vast mass of detail must be learned by rote. It is the ambition of the Chinese to secure these positions. The system is probably one of the causes which has led to the stagnant formalism into which this people has fallen.

Too much detail is destruction ; too little detail is defect. The one ends in a scholastic parrotism in which the mind is deprived of originality and breadth. The other leaves us without any true understanding of anything, and condemns to mediocrity. The wise preceptor will steer between the two.

Some knowledge of nature, a great deal of patience, and a faculty of putting one's self on the physical plane, if the information to be given is physical, or on the mental plane, if the information to be given is intellectual, of the scholar, are requisites for a good teacher. A union of these capacities is far from common. A really competent teacher is well worthy of his hire. A thousand difficulties will be avoided by children so officered. No pains should be spared to give children this great advantage.

It is rare that a child should be forced to study. A child is naturally curious and ever on the quest for information. If the child revolts at receiving information, it is a complete condemnation, either of the character of information imparted, or of the methods employed. A reform should be undertaken out of hand in such a case. Information should always be shaped to the bent and capacity of the child. If instruction be given on a rational plan, with proper incentives, searching to give it in the line of the child's interest, there will never be a question of forcing the child, but rather of holding it back. The need will not be the whip but the brake.

There may be children and there may be times when study should be forced, but such occasions are so very rare, that the rule should be to at once reform the
4

methods which have brought about what must be considered an unnatural condition.

A disinclination of a child to acquire the information
offered to it may be nature's protest as well against the
matter as the method. Some children will not study,
without force, arithmetic, while history is to them a
pastime ; with others the reverse is the case ; they will
take to the arithmetic and hate history. One finds continual instances of this kind. In fact, it is rare that a
child has not affinities and facility in some things, and
aversions and difficulty in others. Children should be
pressed the least possible, and generally not at all, on
what they dislike, and turned freely into that course for
which they show a predilection.

From a child's natural tastes valuable hints may be
derived to show for what useful life they should be
fitted.

The old saying goes, " As the twig is bent the tree is
inclined," a very true and very important fact to bear in
mind. But it is also true that, with favorable natural
conditions, a tree will always grow straight, and always
grow to harmonize and take the best advantage of its
surroundings without any twig bending at all. In a
forest it will, protected by other trees, search with nearly
branchless stem for sun and air ; in the open it will be
·shorter, thicker, and throw out low branches to protect
itself from undue amounts of sun and wind.

Nature, so safe a guide with trees, may well be more
trusted with human beings than it is. Where a parent's

or teacher's care comes in best is in furnishing fertilizers
and cultivation.

To carry the simile of trees to those few children
who may need force and correction to lead useful lives,
let us take the fruit-trees.

Some, like the apricot, should be pruned. It is better
for the fruit that they should be pruned badly, nay,
massacred, than not pruned at all. Others, like the pear,
apple, quince, and most of the fruits, should only be
touched by the skilful, and then but lightly. It is far
better for these, the great majority of fruit-trees, not to
be pruned at all, than to be badly cut to pieces by the
ignorant.

Other trees, then, are like the walnut, that are only
pruned at the expense of fruit-bearing and general
vigor. In my experience these latter trees are much
better in every way when unpruned. They bear earlier,
give larger returns, and are stronger. But all these trees
give great returns to cultivation and judicious care.
The object of all our care to fruit-trees is to obtain
results.

So it may be said of human beings. Some few need
force and correction, typified by pruning, and are better
off, even though the correction be coarsely and roughly
applied, than they would be without it.

Others and many are improved by some judicious
direction in the way of suppressing worthless characteristics or fruitless branches ; these are better untouched
than badly handled. Others, then, are such that you can

only cut into and force their bent at the expense of the individual, and to their injury ; these surely should be let alone.

All, like the trees, respond to skilful and appropriate cultivation.

Our aim, ever clearly to be kept in view, should be results—a future useful life.

All children should be given information and practice in the usages of polite society. Not only should they have good manners, which, as has been said, are based on good feeling, but they should be taught how to come into a room full of people and how to get out of it, a thing not as easy to do well as it might seem. They should also be given at least a fair familiarity with what are called the accomplishments, such as dancing, etc.

If a child be ignorant of the usages of society, especially those children of a sensitive disposition, they will be so embarrassed and mortified on their contact with it, as to give them a horror of polite society.

The energy of young people must have an outlet. If their superfluous vitality have not vent in dancing and any well-regulated custom of society, it is but natural to suppose that this energy will take some other course. Thus a young person may become morbid, unhappy, and even take to vice and low companions, as Prince Henry did to Falstaff.

It is therefore a matter of considerable moment to young people after the age of puberty, and particularly about their mating-time, that they should be familiar with the usages of good society, so as to feel at home in it.

In this way the gregarious instinct which is then strong will find a natural and easy satisfaction in association with the best humanity the world affords. Thus your sons and daughters, at a critical period, will be thrown without effort amongst those most eligible for them as life partners.

There are fashions in education as there are in other things. It will be well to conform in some degree to the fashion of your time in education. Otherwise you will be uncomfortable in your social relations. Never follow a vicious fashion in education, no matter how general it may be, or how uncomfortable its absence may make you.

No special course is laid down. This might be done for to-day, but it seems probable that for to-morrow a plan of this kind, dealing with details, would be likely to bring on a Chinese stagnation. Be fixed in principle and flexible in all else.

There are, however, two studies that all children should take irrespective of their selected careers. These are medicine and law.

In taking a course in medicine, it is not meant that you should go to a point fitting you to be a practising physician, but that a course of physiology, anatomy, including some practical dissections, etc., should be taken, and visits to the hospitals be had.

Health is indeed important, but the healthy too often think nothing of it, until, by the violation of some sanitary law, they suffer perhaps beyond relief.

There is probably no way of impressing the importance of health, and of the observation of sanitary laws, as some familiarity with medicine, and the awful and inevitable results of the violation of these laws. Hospitals show these matters under a thousand different forms, but there is one ward into which all young men should be taken, and that is the one where venereal diseases are treated.

No more impressive lesson can be given to young men of the value of marriage, as a mere conserver of health, than a syphilis hospital ward. The horror and revolt of nature against the prostituting of our reproductive powers will be reflected in the eyes of the witness who sees some of its results. Man alone in the Creation prostitutes these powers. Man alone suffers the inexpressible pain and suffering consequent upon prostitution.

In these hospital wards, also, will be seen what to me is the awful penalty of inheritance. The continuation of the punishment of nature to innocent children, and again to their children in constitutional taints. No one knows how long the expiation lasts.

I can think of no surer cure to the promiscuous prostitution of the reproductive powers, than a ward full of human beings, dying, rotting, and stinking with syphilis while they yet live. Sores breaking out, fingers, toes, noses rotting off, and the intellect conscious of the situation.

The plain truth in this case, as in all others, is the strongest moral teacher you can secure.

Physiology should be taught to all young people, certainly by the time they reach the age of puberty. The most important feature of this study should be the action and grandeur of the reproductive organs. The importance of care and attention in the development and strengthening of these organs should not be lost sight of.

Probably a good way to give this information is by studying at first the reproductive organs and their beauty in the plants, showing that the glory of the plant is in its flower and fruit, that is, in its reproduction. From the vegetable world pass to the insects and fish, then to the animals, then to man. Slur nothing. Teach the truth entire.

It may be thought by some that the delicacy, modesty, and purity of the child, and especially of the girl, will be injured by this course.

Do not let such an error deceive you. It is only necessary to go back to your own childhood for a complete destruction of this idea. If your father or mother imparted to you the grand mysteries of procreation, you will appreciate without further argument the value of the information. On the other hand, if responsible and trusted persons told you nothing, as is commonly the case, you nevertheless learned what the sexual relation of mankind was. The reproductive instinct is the strongest that man has. It is also the most important.

Our thoughts, as we develop, will in spite of everything occupy themselves with this function. If our natural teachers are silent, this instinct will fill us, and does fill young people, with an overpowering curiosity. The result is that we inform ourselves on this, the most important duty of our lives, behind water-closet doors, through vile verses of doggerel, in shamefaced talks with servants or vulgar playmates.

The information thus obtained is almost exclusively of a low, obscene, degrading character. We do not have the slightest glimpse of the grandeur of creation in reproduction. Its value, necessity, and godlike characteristics are hidden and suppressed.

An instinct so strong when completely misunderstood by the young is a thousand times more liable to be misdirected and abused than if it were understood.

As has been said, while man by means of Love has the highest view of reproduction, and by the use of the reason has a capacity for a still higher appreciation of this grand function, he has also in prostitution a lower activity in this regard than any other animal. He can and does sink to a depth of depravity unknown in any other organized being.

What then is the object of this silence on so great a topic, by those whose words could guide the youth from so dangerous a fall and lead him amongst the flowers and fruits of life, where our greatest pleasures lie? It is an ignorance impossible to secure,

Can it be well for a child to hear of these things from inferior or depraved human beings ? To have the door half opened and to be shown the very lowest view of sexual activity that can be given ? No ; the present custom is folly dancing an invitation to fruitless crime.

Children will obtain some view of sex. Their curiosity comes from nature and can not be suppressed. They must learn something of its activities.

If the irresponsible are to be teachers in this recruiting of life, the pleasures will be, or rather are associated with, the abuse and misuse of the reproductive powers, where these pleasures do not really exist, while the responsibilities, dangers, and real joys are left entirely out.

Do not commit an error of omission which partakes of criminal negligence. Tell your children in plain, dignified language the whole story. Explain the pleasure and grandeur of a proper use of the reproductive powers. Tell the dangers, disease, and death that come from their neglect or abuse. Tell the truth, the whole truth, and exaggerate nothing.

One of the things to teach in connection with Physiology is the importance of marriage to true happiness, and to the greatest success of life.

The miserable existence of an old man, a bachelor dozing in his club, a supernumerary laughed at or neglected by the young who have come to control. The childless husband living without family life, in a boarding-house or hotel, dropping out of his pleasures

as age creeps on ; his wife, if she amounts to anything
full of ideas of society, flirtation, or woman's rights
with nothing to attach her to home and no home
to be attached to. Extermination staring his hopeless
existence out of countenance. What pictures may be
made of masquerading misery from the lives of the
homeless. The childless man is either a fanatic, a
nonentity, or a *roué*. If he be wifeless, he usually preys
upon society in one way or another. Spends his nights
amongst forlorn, hopeless, and depraved women, drinking to forget the death'shead that presides at every orgy,
or in some way tries to lose sight of the reality of his
fatal mistake. Or if he be wived and childless, he is still
single in fact with only a better regulated prostitution.
His life in this world can be healthier and longer, but
his end is as hopeless and forlorn. He will die the death
and realize himself forsaken if poor, or toadied to and
flattered by the venal if rich. What is worse company
than a venal toady for an inheritance.

It is not difficult to show the joy of a home full of
children, where pleasure reigns with an object for life
and a future to the parents growing old. Any judicious
man who keeps in mind and before his children the immortality children can give, may have a happy and
joyous home, and this can be shown in any community
by calling your young people's attention to and showing
them the lives of people under your very nose. So also
the miserable emptiness of a childless old age can be
equally illustrated in any community.

In such illustrations from life, many men will be found with wives and children and every condition present for a happy home, and still no home or no such home as man ought to have, and no pleasure from his children.

This should be explained. It is always due to one or two things, or may be partly to both.

First. To the fact that the man does not understand the principles of marriage, and what the man's position in that contract is : that is, that he is and must be head and chief. Or,

Second, to the lack of appreciation either in the heart or in the reason of children.

If one feels that the child of his loins is his worldly immortality, his renewed life, and impresses this on his child, he can never have a quarrelling family where happiness, confidence, and mutual support do not exist.

So also children who know that they are the continued life of their parents, and who have instilled into them the necessity of themselves having children to carry on immortality in its only tangible shape, can never lose a regard for home.

The comprehension or knowledge of the principles of law is of great value. The principles of law are the accumulated experience of mankind of the best way to carry on society. Every man should be familiar with them. Innumerable pitfalls and stumbling-blocks will be avoided by such a knowledge.

This study will show how slowly and tentatively the present laws governing society have grown up and crystallized. The superior races have all gradually developed systems of law that are at least similar in their principles. The security in the results of individual effort, that is property and the encouragement of reproduction by the maintenance of the family, are the foundation of all law. Be sure and found yourself in the principles before going much into detail. Law is perhaps the one subject that demands this course.

Formalism is the besetting danger of organized society. As soon as a people achieves greatness, power, and extended influence, an extensive organization becomes necessary and is developed. Organization is conservative and is never long friendly to progress. It diminishes mobility and tends to stagnation.

Organization is so advantageous, and often so necessary, that its drawbacks are always in the end lost sight of. Its follower, formalism, must be guarded against in the most careful way. Anything is better than stagnation. Formalism in education has long since been a prince. The great advances in thought have been made outside of its regulation pale. Thus science in the last seventy years has made wonderful advances, and has revolutionized both our physical and intellectual lives. But it has only been admitted to the schools during the last few years. Its official recognition, so far, has not added to its true laurels of achievement. It may be that science owes much to the enmity and opposition of the universities in keeping it out of their ruts.

In education we must insist at every risk on maintaining individuality and originality, and our aim should be the proper preparation of the pupil for the greatest work of life—THE IMMORTALITY GIVEN BY REPRODUCTION IN THE CHILD.

OBSERVATION.

This quality is natural in all children. Our present system dwarfs the native capacity in this respect. Contact and communion with nature is the first and best means of maintaining and improving this quality. Nature always tells the truth, and nature, therefore, is the best guide.

Show a child the difference between, and characteristics of plants, animals, earths, rocks, and of all natural phenomena. Question them minutely and systematically on details, and thus habituate them to a close observation of everything they see. We should never cease maintaining, by all means, an interest in the workings of nature. As the child develops, the effect of natural laws should be studied and derived from the details with which the child will, at that time, be familiar. In this way it will be easy to teach the child how to preserve his own physical well-being. A valuable means of obtaining this result is the study of sanitary law and the disastrous results of its violation.

Bad sewerage, bad water, unhealthy avocations, and unhealthy locations—their results in low vitality and high death-rates should in all cases be taught. A child's ob-

serving qualities will thus be strengthened, and his attention directed to these matters of the greatest import to
himself and to his future family. By avoiding these
dangers, his own physical and mental activities will be
greater, and he will be able to avert many sad bereave-
ments in the sickness and loss of wife or children.

Give great importance to this matter. If a child
comes from your hands knowing a good horse from a
bad one—how to tell a good cow, a good pig, a good
tree, good plant, good meat, good provisions, good cooking, and can distinguish the good from the poor in those
things coming under his everyday observation, it will be
comparatively easy for him to develop this quality to an
application to any business in life he may undertake.
The father in teaching these things will learn not a
little himself.

There has been one point that has been reserved till
the last, but it is the most important, and that is how to
tell a good man or a good woman from a poor one.
Physical and moral strength should be a twin standard
of excellence.

In this way a boy or girl will come to have innate percep-
tions of the true in humanity. He will avoid the unsuccessful, and in that most important of all the acts of
life—marriage—he or she will be far' less liable to err
than would otherwise be the case.

When you become a parent you should, by continual
repetition, point out the disastrous results of matrimonial
alliances with poorly-bred people. By poorly bred is

meant those who have poor physiques, poor minds, or, as so often happens, both.

This faculty in your children to recognize strong men and women from weak ones should be so thoroughly founded in reason, as to be above and independent of prejudice. Each person who follows these doctrines may hope that the minds and hearts of their children will be so educated as that they will discard and never think of making a scrub alliance in any business of life.

Matrimony is the most important of all these alliances. If a breeder of horses, cattle, dogs, or poultry will become enraged with a careless person, for even so much as placing an opportunity in the way of his animals for degrading their breed, how much more should we, the reasonable beings who attach so much importance to good qualities in the lower animals, care for and consider the welfare of our own stock.

The quality of observation is inherent in the human being. Give it play, cultivate it, and strengthen the reason by continuous application so that the relation of the truths of nature to life can be applied. Thus will the intellect be developed better than by any other means that you can devise.

The duty of the parent is to lead the child to perceive facts for himself and to reason on them. If you can habituate a child to this, the battle is won. Your child's education is founded on a rock. Nothing can stop it except disease and death. The first of these you will have done much to prevent and the second to postpone.

EDUCATION OF GIRLS.

THERE is no more limit to what a woman should know than there is to what a man should know. Time, capacity, and the appropriateness of the thing taught to make the life of the individual useful are the considerations which should decide our policy in Education.

The capacity of individuals differs greatly. One person whose energy is devoted to acquiring the details of the law would make a good lawyer, but were this energy devoted to the details of medicine as well as of law, the individual might be neither a good lawyer nor a good physician. Another individual with greater capacity might study both subjects and be proficient in each of them, or make one subservient to the other. Thus the study of both subjects in the one individual would be detrimental, and in the other advantageous.

Owing to this infinite variety of capacity in human beings it is impossible to lay down any hard and fast rule, as to what any class of persons shall or shall not study. The extraordinary physical energy of the insane is probably due to the liberation of energy devoted in the sane to ratiocination and its application by the insane to muscular movement. We thus see the disadvantage of an ill-balanced development of capacity. The muscular force of some insane is dangerous and not useful, because the energy that makes its manifestation possible has left the mind without sufficient force to guide and control it. Proper balance must be had.

While the sexes, as such, are quite different from each other in tastes and capacities, they still in their individuals frequently cross into each other's spheres. In fact, it is difficult now to say what these spheres are according to the method of a few years past. In general it is true that the creative power of the mind is largely man's, and the creative power of the body is largely woman's. Of the two, I esteem the power of the woman most important, for in it there is a promise of immortality for the individual, tangible and direct. The difficulty of making an educational limit for the individual is equally apparent when an attempt is made to mark a limitation for the sexes.

The nature of our lives as human beings makes it necessary for us to have children. The person or the race without these has before them a prompt extermination. The female, while enjoying the glory of motherhood, has also from necessity to abstain from doing what she could do were she not engaged in this duty.

The great importance, nay, the absolute necessity of performing the duties of motherhood has developed woman for this function. Her character, sympathies, physique, all prepare her for this duty. The energies

5

which naturally take this direction can but in few cases be diverted to other things of importance, without causing some diminution in the child-bearing capacity. The question to decide in our education of girls is where to draw this line, taking into consideration the capacity of each particular individual with whom we have to deal.

The narrowing of the chest and pelvis in many American women, and the lack of power in about 50 per cent. of those from New England, (Allan) to secrete sufficient milk for such children as they bear, is an indication that the alarming diminution in the native American birth-rate is at least partially due to incapacity as well as to artificial prevention. The lack of desire for children now so frequently thrust into notice is perhaps only a reflex of the lack of capacity.

Dr. Nathan Allan, who has examined this subject and the vital statistics of New England and Ohio connected with it, attributes these changes in the birth-rate and loss of fertility in Americans to our system of life and education. The education seems in his view much the most fatal of the two. The opinion of the American-born women against large families and often against any children, and their growing incapacity in reproduction, is shared by the American-born men.

Many side lights show the rapidity of our deterioration in reproduction. Some of these are the lower birth-rate, small families, incapacity to suckle, late marriages, increased divorce, etc. Hirst, the latest authority on obstetrics, shows that malpresentations in labor are more numerous amongst American women than amongst any others. Next comes France, only a little better, then England with only about half as many, and best of all, Germany with less than one third as many as in America.

The general physique and appearance of American women as a whole, is not promising as to reproduction. They are, as a rule, slight, nervous, intelligent, superficial, and fond of pleasure. They lack earnestness of character, faith in anything, and physical force.

Some of the recent statistics show the changes taking place in New England owing to weakness in reproduction. Here is a sample :

Of those engaged in   agriculture, ¼ are of foreign birth.
  "   "   "   "   fisheries, ½ " "   "   "
  "   "   "   " manufactories, ⅔ " "   "   "
  "   "   "   " manual labor, ¾ " "   "   "

The School Report of Manchester, N. H., of 1887, shows 72 per cent. of the children of school age to be of foreign parentage. In Lewiston, Me., of 6,781 minors, only 1,859 were of American parentage. In Mt. Holyoke, Mass., of 6,297 minors but 843 were of American parentage. A population of foreign extraction is taking the place of the native New England stock and not very slowly either. From an almost universal faith in some forms of Protestantism, we find the dominant religion of New England to have become Roman Catholic. The conversions cut no perceptible figure in the results. It has been produced by, immigration of Catholics, and by

the numerous children of their loins taking the place of
the native stock, whose reproductive powers fail to neu-
tralize immigration and death.

From a universal use of the English language we find
large and increasing numbers using only French. For
instance, there are of these French-speaking people whose
avowed object is to maintain their language and religion,
12,000 in Manchester, N. H., 5,500 in Nashua, 20,000 in
Fall River, and a total in New England of over half a
million persons. At the present rate of change the
French language will soon be dominant in New England as their religion already is.

When we consider that all this supplanting of the native stock has taken place within a short period, and in
a naturally fertile race, that had complete and sole
possession, we must realize that there is something radically wrong. Eusebius, Themistocles, Polybius, and a
number of other ancient writers observed similar conditions in antiquity, preceding the downfall of the races
where they occurred.

Polybius, speaking of the decline of the population in
Greece before the Roman conquest, says that it was not
due to war or plague or famine, but to an indisposition
toward marriage, and an avoidance of children when in
that relation. One of his sentences would apply very
perfectly to our own time. He says, " For when men
gave themselves to ease and comfort and indolence, and
would neither marry nor rear children born to them, or
at least only one or two, in order to leave these rich and
to bring them up in luxury, the evil soon spread imper-

ceptibly, but with rapid growth ; for when there was only a child or two in a family for war or disease to carry off, the inevitable consequence was that houses were left desolate, and cities by degrees became like deserted hives. And there is no need to consult the gods about the modes of deliverance from the evil, for any man would tell us that the first thing we have to do is to change our habits, or at all events to enact laws compelling the married to rear children."

We may say in passing that Polybius' legal remedy is not practical. Prof. Seelye shows that similar conditions prevailed in Rome before its downfall.

The education of the female should harmonize with the essentials of reproduction. The limitations due to these essentials ought not to be lost sight of. We cannot forget that the majority of high type women must reproduce to continue the superior humanity and to do this their information and ambition must be for creation in the child.

This limitation is the only one to consider from a purely sexual point of view.

In the chapter on Sex it will be seen that man is totally incapable of performing the most important functions of woman, namely, child-bearing and child-suckling, and is very inferior in many other matters generally performed by women, such as the care of children, etc.

So woman is equally unfitted for the main duties of man. While some women are capable of child-bearing, maintaining a home, and other duties pertaining to perpetuating the race, and are also capable of achieving dis-

tinction in art, industry, or science, the great mass of
women are not thus capable. Women, sound on the reproductive question, may improve the race by improving
their faculties in the outside fight to be transmitted to
their children.

There are, however, occupations which under no
circumstances should be followed by women, and
against which girls should be warned. All occupations
bringing a pressure upon virtue, in offering temptation
and opportunity for sexual prostitution, are of this class.
Such employments as those of restaurant or hotel wait-
resses and chamber-maids, bar-maids, and theatrical
performers are bad. The theatre, as an occupation for
women, has been condemned, directly or indirectly, by
nearly every moral system of antiquity. The Roman law,
until the time of Justinian, forbade a senator or a distinguished citizen from marrying a woman of the theatre,
and ranked them with common harlots.

The Chinese system of law looks on the theatre as so
demoralizing to women, that, in the interest of morality,
it forbids women the theatrical stage, and places actors
in the lowest of its social classes. Even to a late date
in England female parts were taken by boys, as they still
are in China. So general a condemnation by the thinkers
of the past must be presumed to rest on some foundation
of experience.

In educating girls these general facts should be borne
in mind. Girls should be educated first in such matters
as pertain to their principal activities in life, which from

necessity are connected largely with the home. It is in the home that the woman has the only full opportunity of achieving her greatness and glory, the creation of life. As the husband is necessary for the home, it becomes important first to obtain one and second to hold him.

For the first object a general familiarity with the information commonly given to girls is probably advantageous, together with such accomplishments as dancing, conversation, and music, which attract the man to the girl in social gatherings. It must be said here, however, that the long hours of practice on musical instruments by girls not gifted in music is a clear loss of time and energy without any compensation. No one cares to hear often an indifferent performer strum on the piano. Girls, as a rule, spend many hours in the house, to the injury of their health, on this generally useless work, only to neglect it entirely when married.

An important thing in this connection is for a girl to know how to make the most of her looks, to keep her person neat and clean, dress tastefully, and to be possessed of pleasing manners. Men are often attracted by hoydenish, noisy, and immodest women, and follow them for temporary amusement, but no good man that is good for a husband to perpetuate life is ever attracted to such a woman as a wife. Occasionally, however, they are trapped into marriage by one of this type. Every young woman therefore should be taught modesty and good breeding, and be impressed with the fact that any success of bad-mannered women, and especially of immodest or unwomanly women, can only be either temporary with men seeking amusement, or with men lacking character or information, who will not make good husbands and fathers.   Good looks attract, but it is the charm of good manners that holds.   Beauty is the beacon that brings the beau, but it is manners that hot from the heart may singe the adventurer's wings so that he flies no farther.

Do not misconstrue this suggestion into the advocacy of a cold or prudish manner for girls.   A girl gains greatly by a happy help to some smitten swain, too diffident to take the step to the immortality of marriage without it.

Observation indicates that as between two extremes, a too forward, or a too cold manner, the forward girl will marry where the cold prude hangs on the parent stem.

While the first too-flirty girl finishes at last with a renewed life in a happy row of children re-creations of her life, the over-proper lady closes her story in rooms of a boarding-house, cheered by a wheezy pug, a parrot, or a well-fed cat.

Do not think, on the other hand, that flirting or improper risks of conduct are advised.

But between the frozen pole and the scorched equator take the equator.   At the pole life is dead, at the equator, however disadvantageous or disagreeable it may be, life does go on, and there is a future.

For opportunities in meeting men eligible as husbands, girls are much at the mercy of parental care and their social environment. This last they should make as much as possible themselves. The friendships of youth are formed when the heart is plastic, and, as a rule, are both more quickly made and more enduring than those of riper years. A girl should have girl friends, and these should be in the class of highest mental power, or attracting that power so that her associations as a young lady will be naturally with it. For this purpose a year in a fashionable school may be set aside and sacrificed. It is worth it only in case such friendships are not otherwise easily attainable.

As far as obtaining a knowledge of those things commonly supposed important is concerned, the fashionable institute is inferior to the public school. The life, manners, and language are more polished and polite in the first, but far less strong and sound than in the second.

Perhaps no one thing attracts a good man so much, especially if accompanied by social accomplishments, as a taste for and knowledge of domestic duties and the economy of the household. Men often avoid marriage on account of their fear of its expense.

It is therefore a strong point in a marriageable young woman to not only dress prettily, but to avoid all extravagance. It may be said here that young unmarried women almost invariably look best when simply attired, if there be but a little taste displayed in their combination of colors and the cut of their clothing. To dress expensively is often vulgar, always excites the envy of the small, distracts the attention from the person to the

clothes, and is seldom as attractive as a well-fitted, tastefully combined, and simple dress.

These matters are preliminary to the great object of
life, which in man is the same as in the tree, the plant,
and in the animal world. The main object is reproduction and continuation of the individual and of the species.
But these preliminaries leading to the getting of a good
husband are of importance, indeed, for by their means,
when judiciously employed, the girl is better enabled to
do her part in reproduction, and to enjoy the reward
which the proper performance of this, the greatest function of woman, can give.

In little girls the taste for motherhood should be built
up by dolls, by the care of other children, and by any
other proper means that may be thought of. The body
should be well cared for and developed by exercise.
The girl should have also occupations of a useful character, so as to promote a healthy, moral tone, for it is
idleness that breeds abnormal ideas, premature passion,
and thus leads to vice.

The useful occupations should be, at least to a considerable extent, connected with household duties. A
proper understanding and a proper performance of domestic duties will tend to make her future home better
regulated and happier than it otherwise would be, thus
preparing for the joy and contentment of the future husband and children. She also will feel the good effects
in after years, because the habit of domestic work, and
the consequent interest in home matters, will be to

the wife a great protection against loneliness or discontent.

The second reason why the industries should largely take this direction is that girls cannot be turned out with any safety into the general industries of the world. As has been explained in the chapter on Sex, the penalty of an error is so great in the young girl, that no prudent parent would voluntarily place a daughter in a position where she would be exposed to the temptations which we know are too strong for the great majority of those who are subjected to them. The dangers arising also to unprotected girls, in large cities, is a matter of daily chronicle in our courts. These chronicles are, from all indications, but a mere surface-showing of the extent to which such practices are carried. The ruined lives of a great number of the unfortunate street-walkers of our cities are due to these latter causes.

No young girl should be left in ignorance of these dangers. She should be instructed not only to resist seduction, but to protect herself against force. A woman who will do all she can, by voice and act, to defend herself, need suffer outrage only under combinations of circumstances that rarely occur.

No one should fail to realize that the drift of our society, and of our whole industrial system, is away from family life. Home industries are replaced by general production. The soap-making, spinning, making of clothes, etc., of the old times are largely things of the past in the family. Even fruit-preserving is going out

of the home. Women's industries in the old-time homes
were large and comprehensive. Women in this industrial
change are often left in idleness, or forced into the outer
fight. Woman's increased proportionate contribution in
production is, however, not so great as many suppose.
Here is a difficulty that we should not disguise in the estab-
lishment of a sound family life. The causes of the family
decay at present so prevalent are deep seated and hard
to be sure of. We cannot put a finger on them with
certainty. The growth of one thing out of another, the
interdependence of all social conditions makes it as difficult to appreciate true cause, as it is to appreciate the
eventual results. Extinction and extermination are evi-
dently the results in store for many. How to stem this
dark, strong, and deep current toward family- and race-
death is what we must try for in the education of the
girl.

Nothing can conduce so much to any one's success,
as to be well prepared for the destiny that awaits them.
The destiny of woman being marriage, she should be
thoroughly prepared and educated for its duties, before
any serious invasion of her time or vitality should be
permitted for secondary matters. The girl should
be taught the facts in relation to her own body, and
especially informed as to the care required at coming
to the age of puberty, and during the periods of menstruation.

During menstruation the rule for all girls should be
rest. No severe mental or physical efforts should be

continued at this time ; particular attention should be given to seeing that the girl is attending to the regular elimination of excrementory matter. About the age of puberty, girls become sensitive, and are ashamed to attend properly to these duties. Such a neglect will almost certainly bring more or less suffering in its wake. In his *Diseases of Women*, Dr. Alonzo Thomas gives his experience as to the causes of women's diseases as follows :

" Neglect of out-door exercise.
Excessive development of the nervous system.
Improprieties of dress.
Imprudence after parturition.
Prevention of conception and induction of abortion.
Marriage with existing uterine disease."

Dr. Thomas goes on to say,

" Want of air and exercise, in deteriorating the blood and enfeebling the muscular system, should be classed first among these predisposing causes. . . .

" Excessive Development of the Nervous System : The necessity for a due proportion existing between the development and strength of the nervous and muscular systems has always been recognized, and has given use to the trite formula '*mens sani in corpore sano*' as essential to health."

Girls should be carefully watched to prevent undue nervous development. By care, such a tendency can be observed early in life. When it is seen, the girl should be kept out-doors and physically busy as much as possible, and mental effort should be kept at a minimum.

Dr. Thomas says,

"Unfortunately the restless, energetic, and ambitious spirit which actuates the people of the United States, has prompted a plan of education, which, by its severity, creates a vast disproportion between these two systems, nervous and muscular, and its effects are more especially exerted upon the female sex, in which the tendency to such loss of balance is much more marked than in the male. Girls of a tender age are required to apply their minds too constantly to master studies which are too difficult, and to tax their intellects by efforts of thought and memory which are too prolonged and laborious. The results are rapid development of brain and nervous system, precocious talent, refined and cultivated taste, and a fascinating vivacity on the one hand ; a morbid impressibility, great feebleness of muscular system, and marked tendency to disease in the generative organs on the other.   .

"Improprieties of Dress: The dress adopted by the women of our times may be very graceful and becoming, it may possess the great advantages of developing the beauties of the figure and concealing its defects, but it certainly is conducive to the development of uterine diseases, and proves not merely a predisposing but an exciting cause of them."

Dr. Thomas goes on to say that excessive constriction of the abdomen, or the hanging of heavy articles of clothing on the pelvis, tend to displace the uterus and produce disease.

Dr. A. Sargent has made some experiments in regard to the effects of tight lacing with women. The following is one with his comments :

"In order to ascertain the influence of tight clothing upon the action of the heart during exercise, a dozen young women consented this summer to run 540 yards, in their loose gymnasium garments, and then to run the same distance with corsets on. The running time was two minutes aud thirty seconds for each person at each trial, and in order that there should be no cardiac excitement or depression following the first test, the second trial was made the following day. Before beginning the running the average heart impulse was 84 beats to the minute ; after running the above-named distance the heart impulse was 152 beats to the minute ; the average natural waist girth being 25 inches. The next day corsets were worn during the exercise, and the average girth of waist was reduced to 24 inches. The same distance was run in the same time by all, and immediately afterward the average heart impulse was found to be 168 beats per minute. When I state that I should feel myself justified in advising an athlete not to enter a running or rowing race whose heart impulse was 160 beats per minute, after a little exercise, even though there were not the slightest evidence of disease, one can form some idea of the wear and tear on this important organ, and the physiological loss entailed upon the system in women, who force it to labor for over half their lives under such a disadvantage as the tight corset imposes."

Dr. Sargent's extraordinary success in getting these young women to run a certain distance in exactly the same time under varying conditions cannot escape our comment. His evident enmity to the corset has made his figures somewhat unreliable.

The lung capacity of the individual woman with corsets, Sargent shows to be 134 cubic inches; after taking corsets off, 167 cubic inches; gain with the corsets off 33 cubic inches. The effect of the loss of so much fresh air one would think must diminish the physical capacity and vitality of the woman.

Imprudence during menstruation, Dr. Thomas says, is a prolific source of disease. Exposure to low temperature or inclement weather during this period should be avoided. Imprudence after parturition he specially counsels against, and particularly mentions the pernicious habit of tight bandaging of the abdomen : a well-fitting bandage only tight enough to give support he employs himself, as a source of comfort to the woman. He says these bandages have no effect in preventing deterioration of the figure,

" Prevention of Conception, and Induction of Abortion :   Means
established for the accomplishment of the first of these ends are often
productive of uterine disorders.   This will not be wondered at when
the harshness of some of them is borne in mind.   The workings of
nature in this, as in all physiological processes, are too perfect, too
accurately and delicately adjusted, not to be interfered with materi-
ally by the clumsy and inappropriate measures adopted to frustrate
them.

" The practice is becoming exceedingly common, as every physician
is aware ; so common, indeed, that in the older portions of this
country (unfortunately it must be said in the more civilized and
educated) it is by no means usual to meet with large families of
children.

" All physicians of ability and standing agree that prevention of
conception and abortion afterwards are a certain source of disease."

Dr. Goodell in *Lessons on Gynecology*, condemns
these practices very strongly, as injurious both to the
male and the female.   He uses the following language :

"Such then are my views upon these so-called ' misery checks'
and ' common-sense measures ' ; and I feel that they cannot be gain-
said.   I dare any political economist to show me one innocuous
expedient whereby conception can be avoided.   I challenge him to
name a single preventive plan which will not do damage to good
health or to good morals.   Even natural sterility is a curse : show me
a house without children, and, ten to one, you show me an abode
dreary in its loneliness, disturbed by jealously or by estrangement,
distasteful from wayward caprice or from unlovable eccentricity.

" Depend upon it, gentlemen, there are no thornless by-paths by
which man can skulk from his moral and physical obligations ; no
safe strategems by which he can balk God's first blessing and first
command.   Therefore, as hygienists, if not as moralists ; as physicians, if not as patriots ; as guardians of the public health, if not
as philanthropists ; I charge you to frown upon such practices and
take a bold stand against them.   Else, see to it that in the end you
are not held to a strict account for the knowledge you have this day
gained,"

The opinion of reputable physicians, as far as I have been able to learn, is uniformly that measures to prevent conception are fraught with dangers to health, and that abortion is in the vast majority of cases followed by long periods of suffering and ill-health. The concensus of opinion is that these practices shorten life, make what they leave of it unhappy and sickly, destroy a complete home-life, undermine character and morality, and are physically and financially more expensive than childbearing.

One physician has called my attention to the loss of beauty, both in body and expression, by married women who prevent conception. He pointed out confidentially, several instances of persons known to us both, in whom I would recognize the deterioration. The greatest number of patients seeking relief from specialists in female diseases owe their diseases of the generative organs to means used for the prevention of childbirth. That these cautions are not unnecessary is shown by the works of all modern medical writers on female diseases. According to the researches of the Rev. S. W. Dike, secretary of the National League for the Reform of the Divorce Laws, fully fifty per cent. more children would be born to American mothers in Massachusetts were it not for these practices.

In that State the native American is being replaced by foreign races, for the birth-rate amongst the Americans is in many places less than the death-rate.

Dr. Nathan Allan has given a great deal of attention

6

to these subjects. In his pamphlet on Physical Degeneracy he makes the following remarks:

" Again, connected with this weak and relaxed state of the muscular tissue, and with the above-mentioned effects of fashion in dress, has sprung up a class of very grave complaints which once were comparatively unknown in our country, and are somewhat peculiar to American women. We refer particularly to weaknesses, displacements, and diseases of organs located in the pelvis. Within twenty or thirty years there have been not only marked changes in the type and character of the diseases of females generally, but THIS CLASS comparatively new, has increased wonderfully."

No one but a medical man, who has devoted special attention to this subject, can realize fully the nature and extent of this change, and understand its direful effects. These complaints have frequently been produced, have certainly been aggravated, and sometimes made incalculably worse, by the various means and expedients which the parties have resorted to, in order to interfere with or thwart the great laws of population. It is not in their effects upon the general health, that renders them so important, but the relations which they sustain to the marriage institution, and the laws of reproduction.

Prof. Thomas Addis Emmet, M.D., LL.D. etc., in his _Principles and Practice of Gynecology_, condemns methods of prevention of childbirth, and equally condemns the destruction of child-life before birth. In discussing the effects, pages 24 and 25, he says:

" Can any one, accustomed to treating the diseases of women, say in truth the statement is exaggerated, that we see on any one day more sorrow and misery resulting from the abuse of the marriage state, than would be found in a month from uncomplicated child-bearing."

The effect of education and training both as to these practices and their results is shown by the Jews and Catholics. Amongst this class of the population prevention, abortion, and uterine disease are alike very rare. Amongst them also family life is happier, and divorces fewer than in the general community.

Reason enters most into the education of the Jewish women, and superstition most into that of the Catholics on these questions. In either case the result is the same; large families, happy homes, and a supplanting of the population not sound on these questions.

It must be noted, however, that the Jews are not as sound as they were, and that the Catholic religion does not always lead to the results we see in America. This can be observed by studying the vital statistics of Catholic France. The method of perpetuation of their families, and of education of their women practised in the royal and noble families of Europe, are well worthy of observation. The effect of the system of education of the women in the royal families of Europe is shown by the fact that so few of these have ever been unchaste, and that they make good mothers. The royal families of Europe have been able to resist the destructive tendencies of wealth, better than the families of the rich commoners in the same countries. Women of royal birth who have created scandal by their conduct may be counted on the fingers of one hand. The desire to perpetuate their race, to furnish a scion to carry on the name and power of their family, has been a sufficient

religion to make them good and true women. One element in this system is the care given to parturient women.

Instinct in the animal world is more and more largely
replaced in man by the reason as a guide to action. We
find animals taking care of their young by instinct,
biting off the placenta, washing the new-born animal
with the tongue, providing food of proper kinds, or
suckling them, etc. All this without any previous individual experience or knowledge, doing their duty by
instinct. In man this instinct has become weak as to
details, or has never developed with their new necessities
in civilization. Thus a midwife, a doctor, or a mother
must be taught what to do in order to make the birth
of the babe safe and its subsequent care proper. We
may say positively, that while the instincts leading to
creation and the love and devotion to the babe are strong
in every normally constituted woman, the instinctive
knowledge of what to do in detail, say as we see in the
cow, is practically absent.

Young mothers, in default of a sound education on these
points, often lose or injure their first children and also
injures themselves. The result is sometimes too little
attention for the babe, and perhaps, more often, too much
attention that is harmful. Thus exhausting labor is done,
not only useless but positively harmful to both mother
and child.

A girl should be taught the care of children by practice
and of herself during the period of gestation. It is not
the custom to teach girls these subjects, but the error of

this may be suspected when we consider the general fact that girls, members of large families, make better wives and mothers than girls who have grown up without this incidental instruction in child- and self-care which a large family necessarily gives. There may be some objection to giving such information on the ground of modesty. This point is discussed in the chapter on Education. It is an objection that, however well founded when religious dogmas commanded our obedience and when physiological information was imperfect, has no good and reasonable support now.

It cannot be slurred over in recommending this rather radical frankness that civilized people, as a rule, leave their young in ignorance as to the reproductive functions as long as they can. We would not be wise to overthrow so general a rule without sound reason.

Lately we have become acquainted with the demonstrable physical injury done the individual by the abuse of these functions. Those who favored ignorance on these points, and who have made and upheld our custom of silence in regard to them, had no such information. Consequently silence in their case and the dark closet may be presumed to have been advantageous. It is of course true that so overmastering an instinct as that of reproduction would occasionally break out and rush into the light. Then, dazzled and lost in the sudden illumination of a banked-fire bursting into flame, would rush into an effrontery of excess or, shamefaced but curious, slink behind the commode for some further knowledge of the mystery.

When, besides this new and morality-teaching information we are able to offer to the young an improvement of
self in the child, an immortality of the physical self in
procreation, and to demonstrate the injury to the reproductive power of abuse or excess or wrong of any kind,
nay, more, the prospect under such conduct of extermination and of a complete and everlasting death as far as any
demonstration goes, we certainly offer a motive for purity
such as has never existed.   In the vista of our morality
lies perfection and eternity.

With these changed conditions silence instead of a support is a weakness.   We need not fear light and knowledge, when every ray of light and every bit of knowledge
is an additional information on the advantage of morality
for the greatest greatness, Immortality in the Child.

If a young woman comes to marriage and maternity
with no knowledge of her creative powers, and no practical knowledge of the care of babies and children, she
acquires this information by her own experience.   At this
late date the knowledge thus acquired must be at the
expense of herself, the husband, and the child.   Her
ignorance will endanger the unity of the marriage relation,
the happiness of herself and husband, her bodily health,
and the life of her first children.   It is probably no exag-
geration to say that one half of the unhappy marriages
which pain so much every thoughtful person are due to the
ignorance of the wife, the husband, or both.   Probably two
thirds of the deaths of children between birth and the
second year are due to the ignorance of the mother.

The treatment by young mothers of their first children is often so absurd that it excites laughter in spite of one's pity for the poor little ones. There must be also a very large percentage of the ill-health, of young women and mothers which is due to their ignorance of themselves, and of the processes of nature to which they are subject.

The value and importance of motherhood, its necessity for the perpetuation for her and her husband's life, its value as a hold upon her husband, as filling the declining years of life with happiness, and as a means of maintaining and prolonging health and life in the mother herself, should be the one thing constantly kept in sight in the education of girls.

To have children is natural—not to have children is unnatural. To be natural—that is, to follow what we call the laws of nature—is to follow the path of least resistance in life, and therefore to accomplish the greatest results with the least effort. To follow any unnatural course must cause a great deal more friction than would otherwise be the case.

From these considerations we can understand why it is that married women have a better prospect of life than unmarried ones, and that childbirth, instead of increasing the death-rate amongst women, diminishes it.[1] It is

---

[1] The great insurance companies now making an active canvass for women's life insurance have established rates on the best figures attainable. Their investigations on American and English figures give women bearing children the best prospect of life. They explain it in figures by charging the childless woman, single or married, five dollars a thousand more than the mother.

unfortunate that there are no statistics as to effects of childbirth in marriage itself. But there are some side lights which give indications on this subject. Fifty years ago such a thing as the prevention of childbirth in respect- able families in this country was practically unknown. Abortions were rare. At that period the general sanitary conditions in which women lived were much inferior to what they are now. The general death-rate, and conse- quently the total amount of sickness under similar con- ditions, was much greater then than now. At that time such a thing as a gynecological chair in a doctor's office in general practice was a curiosity. It is now the rule rather than the exception.

The peculiar diseases and weaknesses to which women are now so subject were very little known thirty years ago. These things all point in one direction ; that is, while the general health of the community has improved, the health of married women has retrograded. This retrogression, as far as I am informed, is largely confined to the reproductive organs, or to secondary effects arising from disorders in these functions.

We thus see not only specialists for the diseases of women, but we also find the gynecological chair becom- ing an article of furniture in the office of the general practitioner.

With this diminution in the health of women, we also find a diminution in the average number of children they bear. This diminution of health and of children is pre- sumably due to a common cause—which is the artificial prevention of childbearing. The object of these vile practices is to avoid pain and trouble. Instead of accomplishing this purpose, it will thus be seen that a contrary result has been brought about. Instead of less pain and trouble, these practices cause more suffering. But this fact in reference to the physical results of these practices is only a small part of the truth. The absence of children in a family, and especially their absence through artificial causes—means, as we have seen, increased sickness on the part of the wife, and therefore a diminished inclination and capacity for performing her other duties as wife. The hold on the husband weakens, the pleasures and glory of motherhood are past, and desertion or divorce is too often the ending of all chances to happiness.

The beauty alike of complexion, expression, and youth is longer maintained in the mother than in the fruitless. Childless wives, or those who, having one or two children, prevent or destroy further conceptions, as a rule have a drawn, pallid, and tired look. Premature old age stamps them for this error, and they lose at once the glories of immortality in the child, and their beauties and attractions as individuals in the to-day.

The life of no animal or plant is complete without the flower, fruit, and seed. It is the reproductive moment in life which is the glory of all living things. Man is no exception to this rule, but, rather, being the highest pinnacle of the wonderful complexity of life in the world, is also the most glorious in his reproductive moments. Sterility in man takes from him all possibilities of a happy

or complete life, and leaves him to sink at last in a miserable, lonely, and abject death. From these reasons it
must be evident that the Bible statement of the reproach
to women, which sterility was, is pre-eminently true. It is,
from every consideration, a misfortune and a disgrace for
a married woman to be without children. For every true
man, it cannot but be a continual matter of regret to have
a childless wife. So the rule has been laid down for the
government of my family, that any woman coming into it
as a wife, who has no children within a reasonable period,
must be cast out. For all the intents and purposes of
life, for all the intents and purposes of marriage—she is
no more a woman than a eunuch would be. She might
as well be a block of wood cut in the semblance of the
female.

No matter what advance women may make, and no
matter what turn evolution may take in regard to the
position of the sexes, as long as we have death together
with life we must have reproduction ; and as the impressions of youth are the most permanent and lasting, the
best manner of securing the performance of the reproductive function should be taught boys and girls from the first.

The object of accentuating this subject so much in this
chapter is that the so-called higher and better education,
at this time prevailing, leaves these matters altogether out
of sight, and with girls tends to the creation of habits of
thought and ambitions inconsistent with maternity. The
highest education of the female to-day points her for the
grand prizes of life, to the outer struggle of the world ;

whereas the grand prize of life for either man or woman is the Child—the child better mentally and physically than the parent.

From the peculiar necessities of the case, the woman has by far the greatest influence of the two sexes upon the child. She has also a greater amount of time and energy to devote to producing and caring for it. Her influence upon the child arises from the necessity of her care for it. The time and life energy she devotes to the child indelibly imprints her influence upon it.

No education of the girl can by any possibility be good that neglects these most important of all subjects. To educate a woman and make no allusion to reproduction, to marriage, and childbirth, would be like a description of the heavens without mentioning the sun.

There are two classes of men who see a great deal of nude women—artists and physicians. Artists see women as models. As a rule art is not conducive to morality, artists being notably rather loose on sexual matters. Physicians, on the other hand, make, as a general thing, exceptionally good husbands and fathers, and, with all their opportunities with foolish women, seldom fall away in morals, certainly not more often than the average man as far as common opinion goes. This difference in these two occupations goes to show that nature known to the full, as it is by physicians, is not liable to mislead, while nature seen on the outside, with the glamour of secret meetings, is on the contrary a temptation to error. Therefore the whole of nature should be taught.

There are two races of people only who have made, and
continue to make, the bearing of children a matter of
the first importance.   Equally there are but two races of
people who have maintained their recognizable unity
through the ages of time since we first heard of them.
These two races are the Chinese and the Hebrews.
Consider well this fact—of all the brilliant civilizations of
Assyria, Egypt, Tyre, Carthage, Greece, Rome, not one
has left a recognizable people to perpetuate its greatness.
But the Jewish people and the Chinese people maintain
their vitality and force to this day.

The main point in the religion of the Chinese is, that
the future happiness of man in another world depends on
having a son to maintain certain sacrifices to his spirit
after death.   This principle having been maintained from
the early times to this day, the race has been able to hold
its individuality in spite of famine or plenty, defeat or
victory.   While certain causes have arrested the development of its civilization, the race is ready at any time
for an advance, whereas many civilized people without
this safeguard have disappeared forever, and been
replaced by barbarous clans who were sound on the
question of reproduction.

The Jewish domestic life is admirable.   Few of their
women fall into the horrible *impasse* of a life of shame.
Married life with them is more generally happy than
among any of the peoples with whom they reside.
The cardinal point of marriage with Jews is children,
and the proper care and rearing of them.   Rachael cried

"Give me children or I die." Thus though at fault in some things, and scattered to the four winds of heaven, the Jews by this intimate regard for reproduction have perpetuated themselves from immemorial time, and have seen one civilized people after another die and disappear.

The lesson from these two races is that a people sound on the question of reproduction may consider all errors on other questions as venial, for they may be cured by time. Without reproduction there is but one outcome, permanent death to the race.

Reproduction is therefore the one and only thing to which everything else should be sacrificed.

I refrain from laying down any details in the education of girls. Such a course might lead to the obscuring of the great principle of reproduction which I wish to leave clear and comprehensible. There is, however, one caution to be considered in the method of education mentioned long ago. The translator of the wise Bishop Lugnon says: "Do not allow your daughters to be taught letters by a man though he be a St. Paul or a St. Francis of Assissium—the saints are in Heaven."

The caution is probably against the old method of the well-to-do to educate their daughters separately and privately. In this case they would necessarily be much thrown with their instructor, often perhaps alone. If this be a correct interpretation, the old Bishop was wise and his advice should be followed.

Girls should be educated as highly in body and mind

as possible. They should be made as self-reliant and as strong as possible.

All things, however, should be made and explained to be secondary, and mere incidents of the great duty and glory of woman—which is reproduction, and not only reproduction, but reproduction with improvement.

A wife without children can never be sure of her husband, for the tie that holds them together in sterility is purely artificial. The natural tie is the inseparable union of the two lives in the offspring. The vows of marriage are based on the necessity of giving to man a security in the paternity of his children which would be impossible without chastity on the part of his wife. But the marriage license, the marriage ring, and the marriage vow do not make the bond. The real union is the child. The circumstance and ceremony of marriage, which differ with different peoples and religions, are but the devices of man to make reliable and certain to the male and female, through the security of paternity, the only true bond, that is the child, in which both lives unite.

Girls should be trained to the truth that by labor alone can they hope for health. Health of body, of mind, and of morals comes by work. To have health in full the individual must use her faculties and muscles, and perform the functions of nature, the principle of which is reproduction.

The work of the girl, from the necessity of her nature, must in nearly all cases be limited somewhat as to the kind and to the place where performed.

As to the kind, from the reasons set forth in the chapter on Sex ; and as to place, on account of the necessity of maintaining the girl's virginity before marriage, and of securing the paternity of the offspring to the husband afterward.

The same exposure to temptation and violence cannot, as a rule, be risked with girls as with boys. We are therefore led to the conclusion that the energies and capacities of the girl, at least before her character is matured, should be developed in the home.

Without reflection it might be thought that this limitation would preclude the full development of the girl's brain by high scientific study. No such necessity, however, exists. Besides the possibility of bringing any science into the home, the home duties themselves for their perfect performance demand science and study, and to-day give quite as much opportunity for original research and discovery as any other occupation.

The sanitary arrangements, ventilation, and drainage of the home, are of vital importance, and no mind is too mighty to be occupied with these questions. For instance, in the matter of ventilation, the Foundling Hospital in London and the Monkey House in the Zoölogical Gardens of the same city had some years ago a new system of ventilation applied in them. The result was a reduction of the mortality of the children and of the monkeys about one half ; the reduction being specially noticeable in lung diseases, consumption, etc.

Cooking is a science. Good cooking is the putting of

food through at least a partial digestion, and the combination of one or more kinds of it into an agreeable and advantageous dish.

Food while being cooked undergoes chemical changes. These changes should facilitate digestion. Part of the mechanical and chemical work necessary to the assimilation of man's food is now done in the kitchen.

Owing to the ignorance of our housekeepers as to the fundamental principles of cooking, its chemistry, etc., our kitchen work is done at the best imperfectly, and often the cooking instead of improving the digestibility of the food impairs it.

The economy of the diet is likewise a science. Man requires at frequent intervals food to replenish the waste of his system, and in early life to provide for growth. According to the use of muscle or brain, of force in resisting cold or heat, and to many other things, man's requirements for food vary. So what would be an economical diet under one condition would be an exceedingly expensive one under another. Not, perhaps, in money, but economical or expensive in the expenditure of vital force in securing the requisite nourishment for the body.

The appetite is the guide our instinct gives us. At the Arctic Circle we crave fats and heat-producing foods, while in the tropics, condiments to stimulate the sluggish secretions, together with cooling fruits and farinaceous diets, are what we generally desire.

But in most households the appetite is more servant to the cook than the cook is servant to the appetite. Were this not so it is still true that experience, on which the instinct of appetite is built, was had by the race largely before the cooking of food took its present development. It seems therefore but reasonable to think that scientific study, combining the facts found in experience, would enable us at once to enjoy our food more, and by diminishing the energy required at present to digest it, would liberate so much more force to the improvement of the race.

To arrange a well-combined meal, one at once agreeable and containing the proper amount of phosphates, nitrogens, carbons, etc. required by the activities, climatic situations, etc., of any individual, and at the same time not overload his stomach with useless work, is an art.

It is most probable that a meal has never been eaten that was economically perfect, that is, that contained just the requisite portion of nourishment of each variety required without an excess of any. The feeding of children is equally an important subject of study.

The decoration of the home offers a wide scope for artistic taste, and other things such as music, etc. may be highly developed.

The science of reproduction, the most important with which mankind has to deal, as has been said, is eminently an appropriate, nay, a necessary study in the home. The whole of Anatomy and Medicine are not too much for this one study. To properly bear children, to care for oneself or others before and after childbirth, to preserve the lives of the new-born, and to bring them through many

7

dangers to be fathers and mothers again, these are things
of the greatest import. Every one should understand
them.

Give, when possible, a reward for work. In the first
place, this gives play to the desire to do something, generally found in the young, and connects efforts with results
gratifying to the individual by motives of self-interest. In
the second place, there is in this method an opportunity to
teach girls the relation of the circulating medium to their
own work, and to the purchase of that of others. The
value of money is often never understood by women. The
result of this is usually undue friction in the home, through
bad economy in some directions and wasteful extravagance
in others. A girl should therefore receive a reward for
labor, and should be taught to use such pay for the purchase of those things she needs and desires ; and, further,
should be given commissions to purchase those things the
parents supply for her beyond her own means and also in
general matters. Due care must be taken not to drown
family affection with too cold a flood of business. The
error, however, is so universally in the other direction, that
the caution seems hardly necessary.

The mind of a child is immature ; while more amenable
to truth and reason than to anything else, it becomes
easily tired and discouraged. Ignorance seizes the imagination, and paints so gorgeously the unknown, as to leave
the present life dull and tame by contrast. Therefore,
you should enlist self-interest not only in the often unap-
preciated and distant future, but in the to-day. Give small

wages for cooking or other household work, or rewards of some kind as spurs to effort.

It is wise also to show the girl the hollowness that lies behind the gaudy tints of romance. Imagination generally deals largely with wealth. It will not be difficult to show the girl the emptiness of mere money. Take her behind the scenes of the rich woman's existence so that she can see the truth for herself.

While a young man I spent some time on the then wild western plains, in a geological expedition. We lived in tents, slept on the ground in blankets, lived on bacon and hard-tack with beans and game as occasional luxuries, and worked hard, often rising at three or four o'clock in the morning to commence our journeys. I look back to no period of my unmarried life with more pleasure, or as having been happier. I have always remembered this as a comment on the part wealth plays in happiness. In this connection Colton's saying should be remembered. I quote from memory :

" In estimating the value of money two things should not be forgotten : 1st, that there are some things that money cannot buy and those the best ; 2d, that there are some evils that money cannot avert and those the worst."

It may be even well to show her under safeguards the misery and degradation of a prostitute's life. When one of these at a certain age has come to drink, no more speaking sermon for virtue could be made than the spectacle of her, in her drunken and dirty disgrace.

The life of girls brought up at home has but one disadvantage,—the lack of opportunity through experience and contest to develop self-reliance and character. This being the weak point, much energy should be devoted to counteracting it, not, however, by endangering the value of the home-life which creates the weakness, but by throwing responsibilities on the girl at every good opportunity and by such other means as may be thought of. Under proper safeguards the young girl should be given large opportunity to become acquainted with and used to the presence of young men.

The French system of strict surveillance and seclusion of girls until marriage has not been satisfactory. French wives are not prolific, nor are they noted for virtue. Novels are usually somewhat of a criterion of the morals of those who read them. Judging by this standard the French are not particularly pure in wedlock. On the other hand, the extreme New England system of license to young people before marriage is equally devoid of advantage in securing morality or progeny. A reasonable medium is what is required. A girl brought up with a knowledge of herself, imbued with the religion of child-bearing, and acquainted with the necessity of purity in securing the devotion of a husband, the father of her future children, must acquire additional dignity of character. As she knows the tremendous importance of her destiny as a mother, a perpetuator and improver of herself and of her race, so will she guard her virtue and reputation so essential to make her destiny grand.

THOUGHTS.

THE arch that bears up society in its progress has, as all arches have, a foundation at each end. On one side is matrimony, giving the security of the paternity to children, and on the other side is the security of enjoying the results of labor or the security of property. Both of these foundations have been called on to support off-shoots not in the line of the arch as a matter of beauty or as a matter of strength. On the matrimonial side such aberrations as the guarding and imprisonment of women of the polygamous Turks. On the property side such errors as the creation of monopolies and the inequitable distribution of wealth.

The progress of man involves differentiation, the capacity to improve on what has gone before, and requires necessarily that some individuals should surpass other individuals around them. Nature provides for this by making every living being different from every other. Some therefore must be superior to others or inferior to others, or more commonly, both superior to some and inferior to some.

Mediocre qualitied mankind has ever an intense jealousy of this superiority, which is decreed by nature.

Mediocrity carps at greatness. It recognizes great-

ness only under compulsion. Everlastingly it repeats to
its littleness a denial and skepticism of superiority. When
it catches a great man slipping or falling, it always satis-
fies its repressed feeling by pushing him down or jump-
ing on his prostrate reputation. Mediocrity so much
hates greatness that it will even kick the dead.

Superiority and Inferiority fortunately, when they know
themselves, have none of this. In fact it is almost a form
of greatness when man recognizes that he does not
possess the qualities to make him great. The more marked
however the superiority is, the less jealousy is awakened.
A man first showing unusual mental power is at a disadvantage with his neighbors, who have looked upon him
as no better than themselves. Hence the saying that a
prophet is not without honor, save in his own country.

Humanity moves like the whirlwind in a circle, and, at
the same time, it moves slowly forward. Like the whirlwind, too, the only movement we can see at the time is
that of the circle ; to notice the progressive one we must
look back.

In the circle of human activity error continually
returns. One form of error that invariably drives human
progress back is the attempt to escape the division of
property according to individual effort. The first motive
that man has for work is that he shall be secured in the
enjoyment of the results of his labor. If he cannot have
the fruit of his work, the whole motive for doing any
work is in great measure destroyed. The first step of man's
progress must have been some form of the recognition

of property. As this security diminishes, so is the motive that leads to progress weakened ; as it is increased, so is the motive that leads to progress strengthened.

The complete recognition of individual property is the highest form that this motive has taken. As the results of labor are secure, other things being equal, so is progress slow or rapid.

The ever-recurring stumbling-block in man's progress has been, that, with complex organization, and the power this gives to acquire wealth, has always come an unjust distribution of this wealth, and one at variance with the fair remuneration of labor, or by entails, trusts, etc., removing the motive for labor.

Thus the foundation of every social arch bearing up a past civilization has at certain stages of progress been sapped. Civilization hitherto has always come to a point where it had no strength to resist the barbarian, either at its centre or on its frontiers. When this principle of giving to the laborer his just due and returns for effort is dead, and man has not a proper and fair security in the enjoyment of the fruits of his labor, barbarism seems to spring from the very loins of society itself. It is not necessary that there should be barbarians on the outside, These grow up of themselves, created by the condition of society after it reaches a certain point of wealth. Society in its progress develops tendencies that not only arrest progress but so far have always brought temporary retrogression.

Some speak of the great Roman civilization as having

been destroyed by the outer barbarians. This is ridicu-
lous. The empire, like some old trees, was rotten at the
core, weak and ready to topple over at the least gust,
while still sending out new shoots at its extremities.
Rome died like all great civilizations before it, from
within and not from without.

With the decay of the one foundation there has always
gone on a decay of the other or matrimonial one. It is
not essential to go more at large into this support of the
arch, as the importance of the certainty of paternity is set
forth sufficiently in the chapter on Matrimony.

In the present civilization decay has started and death
has seemed imminent, but Liberty and legal Equality
came, as in the American and French Revolutions, and
saved society.

It must be remembered that while equality amongst
men never has, and while progress is possible never will
exist, still the equality before the law and the liberty of
every man to enjoy the returns of his efforts, at least to a
certain extent, are an essential not only to progress but
to the existence of the highest forms of society.

We have never enjoyed this ideal condition in its completeness. As our population in America grows dense, as
wealth increases, and the free public lands disappear, we
depart farther and farther from it. Every day it becomes
harder for man to escape from the circumstances of his
birth. Some are born rich, some are born poor, and as
they are born so more and more do they tend to remain
irrespective of labor.

Fortunately, there never has been a period in the history of man when work and judgment could not and have not lifted him from the very lowest to the very highest paths of life. No matter what condition society may fall into, remember, my children, this fact—To work and judgment all things are possible.

As has been said, one of the greatest motives for progress ever given man is that he may enjoy the fruits of his labor in his child, or renewed, immortalized self.

Thus inheritance cannot be overthrown. Yet it is inheritance more than anything that fixes men in classes. We all know very well that the rich and the poor do not receive the same justice, the same rewards, or the same punishments for the same work or the same crimes. Consequently the class divisions inheritance does so much to perpetuate are a menace to society. In classes is injustice. Time and time again societies have been built up by the division of the people into classes. Theoretically this system seems, from some points of view at least, capable of great strength. For instance, the ruling class will limit its breeding within its own lines, and ought to produce superior rulers. The Hindoo system is the most striking one of this kind now surviving. Practically, however, class societies have only proved advantageous at a stage of human progress now passed.

It is clear that the full power of the motive inheritance gives demands children. The highest and only complete earthly happiness man has is the family. One of the essentials of the family is children. There is no family

without children. Creation and reproduction is the
crowning achievement of man, as it is that of the flowers,
fruits, and of all vegetables and animals.

Children we must have. Yet it is also clear that
natural increase amongst mankind, unrestricted by the
horrors of disease, famine, war, and crime, would very
soon fill this poor little world with people until not even
standing-room would remain. Amuse yourself for a
moment in calculating the possibilities of human increase,
and see where it will lead you. Remember at the same
time that such conditions never continue to exist, and
that in the top of society the tendency is ever to extermination.

Another difficulty of inheritance is its effect in removing the necessity of labor. In this country most of our
prominent families that leave inheritance disappear in
about the fourth generation. This can be attributed to
the absence of motive for work, the consequent non-use
of the faculties and powers that brought the family into
prominence, and the inevitable atrophy and weakening of
those powers by non-use. This loss of power by non-use
has only to be mentioned to cause every reflecting person
to recognize its truth. Physically and mentally we deteri-
orate and lose power when we do not use our forces.
This danger, my children, I especially caution you to
avoid.

Goods and property are nothing in importance compared to the conservation and transmission of the powers
that acquired them. Without the power, as history will

show you, the property, in spite of everything you can do, will disappear, if not in your children, in theirs.

As an illustration of the effect of the use or non-use of an organ, the experiment of W. Preyer (University of Jena), on the embryo of the land salamander may be cited. The land salamander is a small reptile with lungs and legs. In the experiment the embryo was taken from the egg before it was hatched, placed in tepid water so that it could not get out and breathe the air, and was properly fed. The lungs remained undeveloped, gills appeared and took their place. The legs became atrophied, and fins and a strong rudder-like tail were the organs of locomotion. We here see the normal organs unused atrophy or remain undeveloped, while, on the other hand, changed conditions called forth organs formerly possessed by evolutionary ancestors. The fish in the Mammoth Cave have lost their eyes from non-use. Instance after instance can be given of this. The whole history of evolution is full of them.

Teach then continuously that property while good can be obtained by the able, but cannot be long held by the incompetent. Teach that by use alone can the faculties and powers be maintained. Wealth is a mere incident of capacity. Think and study ever to maintain by use capacity. If you succeed, the wealth will care for itself.

Well-intentioned people are ever perceiving the injustice and suffering to which mankind is heir. So we have prophets, theologians, founders of religions who have endeavored earnestly to lead men so their ills would not occur. It has been in vain. Man suffers still ; injustice still usurps the judgment-seat.

In our own time we have all sorts of efforts going on in the same direction. Each one proving something ; each one, let us hope, doing some good, and doing work that will lead on to the future perfect, immortal race. We have those who say that the remedy is the eating of nothing but vegetables, others that it lies in the drinking of nothing but water, but the most complete and prompt remedy for the ills of man ever preached is undoubtedly the proposed turning of women into men. This idea, if ever accepted, would end the race and its ills with it in one generation.

It is more than doubtful whether woman can equal man in the outside struggle for life which man has thus far carried on. It is certain that she cannot do it and bear children. Childbearing is a handicap in the open fight of life. Coming, as it must, in the most important age of activity, it cannot but place the mother at once at a disadvantage in that fight.

Thus woman, to be equal to man and fill his place, cannot be a mother, and if she successfully competes against him, extermination is the curtain to end the play of humanity.

At this moment Socialism cries out that it alone holds the Key to cure all man's ills. Its first tenet is that all property shall be the State's. The individual can own nothing. The motive for individual effort and labor seems swept away by this system completely. If a man cannot enjoy the results of his labor he has certainly no object in working. Under such circumstances it would be the policy of every man to work as little as he could, and to secure as much of the work of others as possible. The work of the Social State must therefore be done under compulsion.

An incident of the system is that all newspapers, books, publications, etc., would be printed and controlled by the State. Thus criticism of its policies, acts, or even of the improper acts of its officers would have no existence. As the socialist attacks the one foundation of our arch, that is the certainty of man in the enjoyment of the fruits of his labor, so he also attacks the other, the certainty of man in the paternity of his children, and every advanced socialist is an enemy of marriage and an advocate of free love.

Socialism would destroy every motive that has led to progress. Its own picture of a government without critics, without variety, without object or progress, is the most dull, monotonous, and unpromising picture of life I have ever had presented to me. No enjoyment of your own labor, no houses, no children you could safely call yours, free love and no more provision than any other system has for preventing the inevitable pressure of population against the means of subsistence.

Shirking, idleness, and lust governed by uncriticizable tyranny. This is Socialism.

It is an illustration of how little power all our learning and command of natural forces has when any considerable class is ground down too hard and is the victim of injustice.

The oppressed class will fly to any proposed remedy, no matter how unreasonable, if it will but stir up a change. So come police to maintain order that should maintain itself.

While my views are opposed to Socialism in the various forms now proposed, I cannot overlook the tendency of society towards many of its tenets. In fact, this tendency seems necessary for the welfare of society in many phases of its development. What appears to us not in harmony with the principles of human progress may, in better form and with a better population, be a means to accomplish better social results.

All these follies, quackeries, and fanaticisms have their birth in injustice. Where you find fanatics and revolutionists there exists WRONG.

Of the medicines offered to society, and at times forced down its throat, some are good, some are bad, some are prescribed from legitimate inquiry and investigation, others are mere quackeries for the deception of mankind to the benefit of a selfish inventor. Like the medicines offered to the individual, some of the social nostrums do good, others do harm, but not one has been found to avert death. Individuals die at about the usual period in spite of all our medicines. Societies die in spite of all prescriptions. Let us hope that this will not always be so. In the meantime, we must distrust our loud-mouthed doctors and take their prescriptions, if at all, on the homœopathic plan.

Remember in your efforts at improvement that the way

is more by building up the new from or upon the old than in a total overthrow of this. The history of evolution shows us what wonders have resulted from this building process, and how the useless or detrimental may be peacefully and insensibly dropped in progress. The pages of paleontology show us as clearly armies upon armies of living creatures lost and exterminated while confronting too rapid and too radical changes. The history of the English race seems to indicate that a conservative progress is equally best suited to humanity. The evolution of the self government of this race has always been along conservative lines. At the same time, its system is to-day far ahead of that of any other race, although some, like the French, were at times upsetting everything in the abuses of government and apparently leading the vanguard of progress.

Natural conditions have been changed. They are ever changing. Therefore a well-proved natural condition need not of necessity require the endurance of a well-recognized evil. The change of natural conditions, however, must always be along the lines of natural advance. What cannot be resisted or destroyed should be utilized. When societies decay and die, families need not.

Man to live a healthy and useful life must observe certain facts of nature, and live in harmony with them. He must have sufficient exercise, plenty of fresh air, a nutritious diet, sleep, rest, etc. As it is with the individual so it is with society. Certain natural laws must be observed if the society is to have a healthy and useful life, with

strength to reproduce itself improved. Amongst these
laws is that one which demands that man to work and
progress must have a distinct, individually tangible
motive. The two great motives, as we have seen, without
which the further development of man is impossible, are
the certainty of the paternity of the children, and the certainty of man in the enjoyment of the results of his
labor.

No civilization has existed without these. For progress,
the first must be complete with a modicum at least of the
second. The second never has been complete. When
it does so live, it may be that the key to permanent prosperity will be found.

In the knowledge of nature we progress. We study,
investigate, discover. We potter about the locked door
of nature, that is the immediate limit to our view of the
first cause, to find that the key has been laying under our
noses all the time. This door opened we have progressed,
but we are again in immediate presence of a door that
shuts out the view of the first cause as completely as
before.

Let us hope that the solution will soon come. In the
meantime we must work in harmony with the facts we
know and may discover. With patience and a conscientious search for truth, truth will be found.

If the future glory of the race is to be enjoyed by us,
we must reproduce. We must have children, and thus
send our vital flame of life, our own identity, marching on
to future perfection. Never, under any circumstances, lose

sight of this fundamental necessity of human life and human progress.

Human nature has been substantially the same during at least the historic period of man's existence. The motives actuating man to good or evil have not changed in their natures. Periods of virtue have been succeeded by periods of vice ; vice has been supplanted by virtue ; prosperity has been followed by distress, distress by prosperity. Sometimes self-sacrifice, patriotism, and bravery have been dominant, again selfishness, treachery, and cowardice have been most prominent. Still human nature in these changes has remained the same. The differing conditions of society have been due to differing motives actuating man.

Thus you will perceive, my children, the vital importance of always keeping before you the grand motives leading to effort, courage, and progress. The motive makes the man.

A French proverb says, *Ce n'est que le premier pas qui coûte.* It is true that the first effort to do anything whatsoever is the most difficult, and requires the most energy. Each repetition makes the thing done more easy. The subordinate machinery of nerves and muscles act at last without conscious effort. This is most completely illustrated perhaps in piano playing. The beginner has to observe and think of the motion of the fingers and the position of the keys while reading the music. The accomplished player thinks of neither fingers nor keys. His fingers act with wonderful rapidity and accuracy. What is true of

8

the nerves and muscles is doubtless true of the brain. Whatever train of thought we set up or permit must make its repetition easier. Such modes of thought or mental action as we become habituated to at last become a part of ourselves and may be presumed to influence ourselves ·renewed in our children. Consequently, the importance is evident of cultivating in the mind's action as in the bodies, the good, the useful, and the high, and of avoiding the bad, the useless, and the low.

While it is true that man naturally possesses reproductive powers that would, if fully exercised, carry population beyond any power of the earth to support it, it is also true that these powers are never fully exercised for any length of time.

The savage and barbarian overcomes the natural possibilities of increase by female infanticide, which custom, prevalent in China, exists in our own great cities as to both male and female infants to an alarming degree.

But aside from this the development of society has thus far been accompanied by a diminished power of reproduction. This result of progress has been further increased by a diminished desire, especially on the part of women, to have children ; and the consequent practice of preventitive measures, to which late marriages add additional force.

Marriages are growing later in all European countries by statistical evidence and in this country by common observation. At the same time, in cities at least, there is a premature development of sexual feeling. Both are bad signs.

The attitude of society toward marriage and the sexual relation is changing. Divorces and separations, recently rare and fatal to social standing, are now more common and are looked upon more leniently. Prostitution, once only known in this country in the slums, now exists in all parts of our cities, and is tolerated. Prostitutes buy in the best stores, walk on the main avenues, and no longer feel driven either to shrink from observation, or put on a brazen assumption to cover their impossible position.

Prostitution, fatal and deadly as it is, has become in our demoralized civilization almost a respectable business. This degradation and ruin of the woman goes hand in hand with another degradation and ruin of women accomplished by abortion. This is the killing of conceived but unborn life, the killing of her own renewed self, the killing of her hold on the future. It is usually followed by disease of the reproductive organs. Thus outraged Nature strikes back.

This strange suppression of the grandest function of humanity, its power of self-perpetuation, is doubly strange, occurring as it does for the most part among the women and amongst the well-to-do. The race, to exist, must reproduce. For this reproduction, women must be mothers. When they are mothers they are practically out of the world-fight, and must depend on men for that part of life's struggle. The destiny of the majority of women must be motherhood, and the necessities of mothers must and will govern the destinies of the sex. It is therefore clear that humanity must disappear, or women must de-

pend on men for the outside contest of life. There is no
way for a woman to permanently hold a man, except by
giving him children, and perpetuating the combined lives
of the two creators, father and mother. It certainly is not
the desire of the reasonable, nor should it be the policy
of the statesman, to encourage the reproduction of the
diseased or incapable laggards of society. These indeed
breed too much. In their weakness and thoughtless irre-
sponsibility they are in a measure protected against the
extermination that would benefit the world. They breed
because they do not think. The rich or capable think
in a little and incomplete way, and so refuse the trouble
and responsibilities of the greatness of reproduction.

It is the rich and the well educated who either can not
or will not have children. As societies become rich and intelligent, they tend to disappear through sterility. They
have fewer and fewer children, and at last the breed dies
out.

Idleness is born of prosperity. Prosperity exterminates.
Labor alone breeds. Remember this ; guard this point
more than any other. Breed you must ; to breed, you
must labor ; so labor you must. Idleness is death ; kill
it before it kills you.

Labor is ennobling. It has varying advantages according to its character. Every one should commence
with common labor, but should aspire to the highest.
Inferior occupations should not take too much time.
They are useful only in youth, when the faculties are
undeveloped. A command of detail is one essential of

greatness. It should not be allowed to diminish the other, that is, the command of generalization. Very often men in high place have been lost from their incapacity in detail, quite as often they have been lost from an incapacity in generalization. Louis XVI was a good locksmith but a poor king. Many of the Roman emperors who failed in a military epoch were personally skilful in the use of arms. It may be said here that the command of detail comes best by constant contact with the world, while the power of generalization comes in solitude. Thus a man to be great must mix with the world at times, and at times be alone and free from it.

The tendencies of civilization are more and more to the industrial type and away from the military. This does not do away now with the necessity of military knowledge for defence. It may be a long time before organized war is done away with. Even when this happens there seems little prospect that the contest of life will be less bitter and destructive than it is. In fact, philosophers claim with some color of reason that the life contest should be cruel, so that the inferior may not survive to clog progress.

Industrial, as contra-distinguished from a pastoral or intellectual life, is the least likely to maintain a martial or adventurous spirit. Consequently, industrial nations are those at once the richest and the most often conquered. Their riches tempt the spoliation which their cowardice makes possible. On the other hand the industry civilizes and advances, and the superiority of learning and invention has always been a characteristic of industrial societies. These powers may counteract their weakness in military feeling.

Civilization has so much increased man's power that he has come to consider dangers from the exterior as naught. It is probably true that our destruction must commence internally, but such vast populations as those of India and China, when once weakness comes to us, may easily form the nucleus of destructive, emigrative invasions similar to those of the past. We, like the ancient peoples of Europe, or even like our own Indians, may be swept away and the land of our birth know us no more.

Industrial nations, as well as individuals, should remember that it is easier to overcome the obstacles of poverty than to resist the enticements of wealth.

In considering matters of military defence, it may be useful to recall the tendency through history to a return in warfare from book science, strategy, weapons injurious at a distance, and diminished necessity of personal bravery to courage, short weapons, and lack of science.

To maintain a spirit equal to an emergency of war is indeed important. To do this the exercise for bodily health should be of a character to develop courage, self-reliance, initiation, and combination. A game like football does this. Many small things may also prove useful in building up decision, which is an essential in military life. A little rule like this is good. When you go to a barbershop, take the barber you want and not necessarily the barber who wants you. In this, as in all other matters, we should be constantly on the watch to improve and become stronger.

We should never fear criticism from the outside ; we should invite it. Criticism, a spirit of searching always for defects, is so universal as to be presumably useful. We look for the defect to do away with it and improve. While one should be ever alert in this matter in things, methods, children, and self, the spirit of criticism should be kept one of reform, and in small matters of social intercourse should be suppressed.

When you speak of a person, casually speak of their best qualities and forget their defects. Your hearers will remember this treatment of the absent, and feel themselves safe as to tongue-thrusts when they also are away. There is plenty of spice in picking people to pieces in a gap-eared circle. The listener laughs at the cuts and slashes, but trembles to leave his own reputation in your hands. The success of the slanderer makes no friends. It leads to nothing. Leave this business to others.

While labor is essential, rest is also good. In cold countries the climate more or less stops work in winter. In such countries not too cold, where science has overcome the more notable drawbacks, such as the continued expenditure of vitality to resist the cold, the strongest civilization now exists. The question may be asked whether this is not due to the temporary cessation of work in winter. Even if work be continued, it is usually of a radically different kind at the different seasons.

The greatest fertility and vigor in the human race, orig-

inally in the temperate to warm zone, has with the increase
of man's power over the elements moved to the temperate
to cold zone. The causes of this are obscure ; but the
reasonable rest offered the agricultural masses in a cold
winter may be some element in it, when connected with
the relief from the excessive cold architecture and science
have introduced.

It is well to recall the fact that science has done little
or nothing to alleviate the drain on human vitality hot
climates cause. Consequently less improvement has
taken place in these than in the colder climates, and less
advantageous change is to be anticipated.

In delicate health rest is good. Some repose and time
for reflection, so that one can grasp the generalizations
which everyday details drive from you, is very good ; but
do not let repose lead you into idleness.

To wear out is longer in bringing the end and better
every way than to rust out. Idle people are both miserable and mischievous ; avoid them always from youth to
age. Never on any account be one yourself.

A political saying is that the enemies of to-day should
be treated as though they might be the friends of to-morrow, and the friends of to-day as though they might be
the enemies of to-morrow. This is a good maxim when
taken with limitations. Always be a true friend and be a
hot enemy while enmity must be. To the extent that you
are a true friend, friends will be true to you. Not each
one, but the average will make up for individual delin-
quencies.

Nearly the contrary can be said of enmity. A hot enemy, other things being equal, will have fewest enemies, and strangely enough it is the hard hitter and the full-blooded fighter who re-establishes friendship or turns enemies to friends quickest.

A fighter with diplomacy will never lack friends. Avoid getting on the wrong side of questions. When in business or a profession be careful to be right before going into important matters. As a lawyer, for instance, never take a case which you believe unjust, never undertake to set up a doctrine you believe untrue. This course will have its inconveniences, and will at times cut off some paying business. It is quite certain that a man is never at his best in contending for a cause in which he does not believe. It is equally certain that a man who defends only what he believes to be true and just will add great force to his character. He will be a stronger man than he otherwise could be. He will achieve success where he otherwise would not.

Besides all this, such a course must command the respect of every judge, public officer, and citizen, and the confidence of every jury. The eventual outcome of a man's career so ordered must be success. The trouble and disadvantage will only be while he is making his determination known, and by acts securing the belief of the incredulous world in a very unusual rule of business.

Æsops Fables are excellent for study. One of these fables has for its subject a wager between the Sun and the Wind, as to which of them could most easily take a

cloak from the body of a certain wayfarer. The Wind
tried first. It blew strong, then stronger and stronger.
The wayfarer only wrapped his cloak the closer. So the
gusty, noisy, violent Wind failed. The Sun, coming out
calmly, smiled with warmth upon the scene. The wayfarer, soon perspiring, loosed his cloak, and it was not
long before he took it off altogether.

Generally, in life, you will find firm good-nature similar
to the quiet heat of the sun, the best means by which to
accomplish your ends. It is always better than bluster.
The heat of the sun may be fierce and terrible as well as
smiling. It may be destructive as well as life-giving, yet
its forces, as we know them, are calm and regular. They
are the creative and life-giving power of nature. It is no
more trouble to saunter and smile in the sunshine than
to shiver and scowl in the shadow.

Be firm; never be rude; never do little disagreeable
things against even your worst enemy. Do not have
scolding or hair-pulling contests. It is, of course, often
necessary to strike. When such times occur, get your
plans in harmony with your objective point, and when
you strike, strike home. You will always find it easier to
re-establish good-feeling with one whom you have seri-
ously hurt or injured, rather than with him whose nose
you have pulled.

Therefore avoid all little, mean, nagging, disagreeable
things. Be a friend if possible; neutral if this cannot
be, and an enemy only on necessity. Go into no fight
without the intention to win. Fight to win. When you

succeed take the spoils and legitimate fruits of your victory. It is not a very wise course to go beyond small things in self-effacement.

No one can hope to achieve success who does not force some from his path and take the right of way from others. While success involves opposition and friction, judicious management may reduce it to a minimum. Thus a wheel upon its spindle, oiled or greased, will revolve with a friction so slight as to be imperceptible, while the same spindle without the lubricant will increase so much the friction as to eventually heat and stick the wheel and spindle together, so that motion is arrested and a permanent injury done to both. The oil of good-humor is a lubricant that will aid the revolutions of the wheel of fortune. So industry and judgment will not be held back by unnecessary friction.

Fight as little as you can. You will find fighting a small need if you mind your own business. To mind your own business is a course that will keep you out of a thousand difficulties. I very heartily commend it to you.

The motto " Faithful and true " should be your guide in all things, and especially in friendship. Make a business of acquiring friends. A little favor at a critical moment may give you a devoted friend. Therefore look for such occasions. You must not, however, sacrifice the interests of your family to outside friendships. The blood tie always comes first, the friend next.

Go on no man's bond without security. Endorse no notes without equivalent. Make these your rules, and you can refuse a friend upon the general principle. I have an agreement with my brother to go on no man's bond without his consent ; and he is equally bound to me. This is a good idea, and saves one from temptation to do a dangerous act.

Short accounts makes good friends. When you lend money to a friend, count it as lost. Never lend in a friendly way what you must have back. The getting of it back will break the friendship more probably than a first refusal. In selecting agents for the execution of your plans take the young. A man over forty rarely improves ; while a man of any mark at twenty-five almost always does. In the first case you have an agent whose capacities must he presumed to be stationary or retrogressive, and in whom initiative is every day decreasing. In the second case the presumption is in favor of greater capacity and power, and increased initiative and energy. As for contented persons never employ them except for routine work. The contented are of no earthly account in progress. Discontent is our spur in life. So look for the ambitious as agents. Ambition is the word for the highest form of discontent.

In all your acts or schemes lay your plans carefully. Spend time or money or both beforehand to know what you are about, and use ever some special means to keep your main object in view, lest in a long and exciting contest you lose sight of what you are working for. It is the oblivion of their object that forces so many in the world into failure.

Happiness, power, long life, and above all a family for the future are the real objects. The world is full of those who never get beyond the means of attaining an object because they cannot see beyond these means.

Money is a means of attaining certain objects. In itself gold coin is nothing ; it is good for what it will get, yet many think of nothing and work for nothing except to pile up bank accounts, and are in fact never happy, die early, and have no children ; or at best leave some with the poor constitution born of too sordid indoor work. So, having the means, never attain a real object through not having a clear idea, or perhaps having no idea of what they were really striving for. Do not loose good chances by undue delay for preparation. This fault has ruined many generals.

Do not give up your individuality, or your legitimate objectives. These, however, can be best attained by an examination and study of the conditions surrounding you, and by working in harmony with these. "A wise man is like water ; he can fit himself to the shape of any jug."

It would not be wise now to put on armor to go to war, but it once was. It would not be wise to eat whales' blubber in the tropics, though it would be wise to eat it in an Arctic winter. So times and conditions vary ; according to these you must choose your means, being ever mindful that truth is essential in all your dealings to preserve your own character and your own greatness.

Your own force is what you must depend on, if not to achieve position, then to maintain it. Your force will depend on your own self-respect and self-reliance. Every departure from truth injures these, hence the necessity of truth as a guiding star in your lives.

It is said of Henry IV., of France, that he adopted the policy, in harmony with his character, of telling the truth in his diplomacy and State affairs, and confounded his opponents thereby.

There is one person with whom your are always—this one is yourself. If you have a scrub-liar and cheat always at your elbow, in every confidence, whispering weak evasion to every enterprise, what a handicap have you fixed upon yourself ! If, on the other hand, your inseparable companion is honest, true, and courageous, and stands to frown upon all that is despicable, that circumstance may suggest, and to counsel high courses of life in opportunity or emergency, what a guard and friend you have ! Do not forget then, that a low act or even thought must lose to yourself your own self-respect, while high courses will give confidence and courage for the future, in the good favor in which you will hold your own soul.

Some carry heroism to extreme. In a fire, for instance, they will burn if some one else cannot be saved. In other cases a person could swim ashore in an accident at sea, but will remain to certain death because some one whom they cannot save is unable to do so. A useless sacrifice is folly.

Character and force can never exist without self-reliance. Self-reliance cannot long exist, if it can exist at all, without individual responsibility. Therefore, all coddling, whether of friend, family, or government, is bad.

This should not prevent aid being given to make individual effort more effective, nor prevent opportunity being made for the beginner. The policy should be to throw responsibility on the one we would see advance, and thereby give play to the faculties of our *protégé* or to our child.

A forceful man can recover from any blow of fortune, except the loss of all his children, in his old age. Thus force is the essential. Wealth, success, or position are mere incidents.

Mental force, with a physical force to carry it, must come to the front ; it cannot be more than temporarily beaten down. Like a cork in water it will come to the top. I speak of these two forces as different ; so the world looks at them. It is, however, clear that there can be no manifestation of intellect without the physical aid of a brain, its nerves, its sensory ganglia, and a member or members of the body, such as hand or tongue, to register it.

A person with no brain can show no intellect ; a person with no members is equally impotent. While only the total absence of brain or members reduces a being to a zero, it is nevertheless demonstrable that an injury to the brain structure, or to the members, must, to the extent of this physical injury, diminish the power of the intellect as far as human life is concerned.

Thus, if the brain be too small in construction or simple in its convolutions, as in the brains of idiots, the manifestations of intellect become less. If the quantity of the brain be diminished by accident, as in the case of the New England man who had a rock-drill driven through his head by the unexpected explosion of a supposed dead blast, and survived with diminished brain-power, or injured as by alcohol, according to the importance of the brain matter removed or injured, so will the exhibition of intellect decrease.

Whether a deficiency of the brain be natural or arti- ficial, it cannot but be accompanied by a deficiency of intellect. The condition of the brain matter, its efficiency and power for work, depend on the condition of the blood it receives and on the general vitality. If a man be dead, no matter what the size of his brain, no manifestation of intellect can take place from him. Any disease or physical inability which approaches a man to death must according to its importance decrease his mental capacity. So the health of the brain and its capacity of exercise depends on the health of the liver, stomach, and of the vital organs, as well as upon the normal activity of its own structure.

Two things are deducible from these facts :

First. The necessity of bodily health and force for the full and healthy use of the brain.

Second. The importance in marriage of breeding to a mate with a brain capacity sufficient to insure good intel- lectual manifestations.

The experiments in the New York Reformatory with

exercise, regular diet, and occupation, have had a more beneficial effect on the morals of the inmates than anything heretofore tried. The result of these experiments show the intimate relation of bodily health, in which I include the health of nerves and brain, with morality.

Exercise, occupation, and a regular life promote health and consequently morality. The thoroughly healthy man is a moral man. Ill-health endangers morality. Immorality certainly destroys health. The one reacts on the other.

In this connection it may be well to call attention to the inadvisability of selecting an unhealthy location or vocation for your activities. It is rare that an increase in pay ever compensates for the difference in risk between healthy and unhealthy occupations or places. In unhealthy locations, in fact, the compensation generally is, or soon becomes less than it is for similar service in healthy regions. The risk to health is the last one a man should take. It not only effects him but him in his children, and he is thus handicapped in the contest of evolution.

A malarious region or one unhealthy from any cause should be avoided. No pay that you will ever receive can compensate you for the risks you run.

It is in such regions not a matter of risk, except as to a positive break-down, but a matter of certainty that your general vitality will be lowered and your force diminished. Climates or conditions in the evolution of man have made him Black, Yellow, Brown, Red, or White,

9

have given him resistance of malarial fevers in one place
and resistance to pneumonia or consumption in another.
Thus the White, going into the tropics, dies of malaria
and liver troubles and of fevers, such as yellow-fever, in
much larger proportion than the dark natives, long since
well weeded out of susceptible individuals. The Negro,
on the other hand, going to the north, dies more frequently than the White from pneumonia and consumption for the same reasons.

Climate is not everything in man's activity, as some
suppose, for we find not only the lazy in the tropics, like
the Tahitians, Hawaians, Negritos, Ashantees, etc., but
the industrious like the Fellahs, Indian Ryots, Mexican
peasants, etc. Vitality and activity seem largely due
however, to climate and situation. Thus swamps, towns,
tenements, etc. are bad, but, as to their effect on activity,
may be neutralized by some artificial condition furnishing a motive for effort. Greece, in its present social and
political inaninity of decay, has a climate doubtless but
little changed from that prevalent during its period of
glory.

Human greatness is then clearly not a matter of climate
alone ; nevertheless, the great civilizations of man have
not arisen south of Egypt, nor north of the Arctic Circle.
Consequently, it is reasonable to say that great continued
heat or excessive cold is unfavorable to man's progress,
and such conditions should exclude a locality as a place
of residence. Everything else being equal, the climate
that causes the least strain on man's constitution and is

still sufficiently unfavorable to plant life to demand industry in agriculture is that in which the greatest progress,
may be expected to take place. The greatest progress
heretofore has taken place in such climates. The shores
of the Mediterranean have an equable climate, but one
too dry for agriculture without constant effort. England
has an equable climate, but too moist and cool to be productive without effort. In tropical islands we have equa-
bility, but plant life, perhaps, is too luxuriant and
productive for the best interests of man in progress.

The line of best climate may be moving northward on
account of the power civilization has given man to neu-
tralize excessive cold. Cold climates seem to encourage
and even produce energy ; for the northern man in this
respect surpasses the southern in every country, and in
many cases this is true of the countries themselves. The
Piedmontese is more energetic than the Neapolitan ; the
Catalan than he of Malaga ; the Alsatian than the Pro-
vençal ; the North Irishman than the man from Kerry ;
the Scotchman than the Cornishman ; the Prussian than
the Bavarian, etc. It is a general rule with numerous
exceptions. The best climate for a permanent residence
would appear to be an equable one, leaning to cold.

A good rule for the situation for the residence is never
to place it in a narrow valley. My rule, while on a Western camping expedition, was never to pitch a camp in a
swail or low place, no matter how convenient it might be.
This was on account of the naked watersheds in that
country, from which a diluvial rain descends with a sud-

den volume destructive to everything in its path. While our watersheds elsewhere are still forested there is less danger, but they are being rapidly stripped or burned off, making them as little capable of absorbing or detaining water as those of the arid west. In other places dams may exist or be built at the headwaters of such valleys. These frequently burst as did that in the Conemaugh Valley. This accident destroyed millions of property and three thousand five hundred lives, all situated or living in this narrow valley.

Every year we hear of dreadful holocausts of this kind. It is a simple matter to avoid this danger by not building or living in a valley subject to inundation.

Unhealthy vocations should be avoided on the same grounds. There is nothing that will compensate a man for the loss of health in himself, as it undoubtedly will be transmitted to his children. The importance of this may be understood by an examination of the death-rates in vocations. Samuel Royce says that the tailors of London show a death-rate 57 per cent. higher than that of agriculturists, and the printers of the same city are said to have the remarkable excess of death-rate of 117 per cent.

In an electrical workshop in Paris thirty-two of the thirty-five workmen were found to have consumption. Many of them contracted the disease in this shop, while many of the others may be presumed to have contracted it in the same line of work.

Exemptions of soldiers in French recruiting show also great differences due to occupation. These vary from

an exemption rate of 46 in the hundred in agriculture to
83 per hundred in scholars.

The very bad sanitary effect of sedentary scholasticism
is here made apparent. The exemption of the scholar, by
the Misna, from any marital duty indicates weakness in a
still more important line. Sanitary conditions are therefore of the first importance.

First. The healthiness of the locations chosen should
be certain.

Second. The drainage, disposition of refuse, ventilation
of buildings, etc., should be looked too so that the health
of the place naturally may not be done away with by artificial means.

Third. The health of the body should be maintained
by exercise and occupation.

A sedentary life, which is idleness of the muscles, or a
lack of occupation, which is idleness of the brain, is ruinous in either case to the part affected. Injury to one
must react upon the other. So a man cannot ruin and de-
grade his muscular system, without injuring not only his
general health, but his intellectual capacity with it, and
conversely, injury to the brain or its degradation by idleness will destroy the co-ordination and effectiveness of
the muscles, and result either in early death or a weak
progeny or both ; the end being the extermination of the
family.

Therefore undue use of either the brain or the muscles
to the neglect of the other should be avoided. Our development must be on the brain road ; the muscular

exercise is consequently mainly useful through the necessity of a healthy body to carry the brain.

A look back at the recorded experience of mankind shows that the great reforms from which progress took new life have very seldom originated or been maintained by the class in control at the time any reform originated. The knowledge of the day has generally been able to make a good case, showing that these innovations were either bad or altogether impossible.

The knowledge of the day was wrong. The lesson to be learned from this is that a controlling class is ever in danger of becoming a slave to routine. The rich by inheritance become rut-bound. The comfort of their position leads them to oppose change, and they take little trouble to examine proposed reforms. Scholastic writers in the hope of gain defend this conservatism, and ease the conscience of the wealthy even upon the most absurd propositions.

Change and new conditions, more than anything else, lead to a development of the brain. So we find the world's outbursts of intellectual light to have been accompaniments of great changes in the conditions of the societies in which they occurred. These changes have often resulted in placing the top class at the bottom and the bottom on top. The importance of watching for new movements and new reforms must be clear. If you wish to improve you must progress, and, therefore, more for your children than for yourself, you must be ready for change.

You should make it a policy to try change and to be habitually reformers. Always seek out improvement, never be satisfied with what is. The present condition of mankind is a misery. Its only mitigation is that it is a stepping-stone to something better which the progressive may enjoy in their children. Families, tribes, and races of men have disappeared and been exterminated, and many of those now existing will be annihilated, and so will you if you fall behind the wave of evolution. By universe time it will not be long before the earth will be uninhabitable to the present type of man. I cannot bring myself to think that all this earth's evolution is to be swept out of existence and go for nothing ; on the contrary, it seems to me more probable that evolution will continue, and that the future man will be at last as far ahead of the present man as he of to-day is above the grubbing worm.

I therefore, my children, commend you to a radicalism with reasonable conservatism keeping sound on the reproductive question until the race rises beyond this necessity. At this time, if it come, what I have written will be left unread. But the reproductive capacity, as man is now constituted, you must carefully guard.

In the improvement of fruit many good varieties have been obtained by the care of man. Of these, not a few are weak in reproductive power or quite sterile, such as the seedless Navel orange. These depend for their continuence upon the artifices of man, such as grafting, etc. Such fruits left to themselves would promptly disappear

through this radical fault. Another point is that when
the reproductive power ceases, improvement also ceases,
and no further advance is ever possible even though life
be maintained by artificial means.

In several places I have spoken of nature and warned
you not to violate her laws. This is very good advice, but
it needs some explanation. Persons often speak of nature's laws as though they understood them very well. I
disclaim any such knowledge. Very little is known about
nature. The little information we have is but a smatter-
ing, a surface skimming from an infinitesimally small area.
What laws we have found may be modified, we know not
how, by other laws of which we do not yet dream.

My knowledge on these points, my children, is unfortunately really nothing. You must not fall into the error
of receiving all I say as unchangeable fact, for you, then,
like so many seeming wise people, would be but the slaves
of authority. It has been my aim mainly to call your attention to the possibility of an earthly immortality through
your children and descendants, and of a probability of a
continuation of evolution to a perfected and self-sustain-
ing race. Your only means of partaking of such future
life is by reproduction.

In being radicals, and studying and working ever for
improvement, do it as far as your capacity will allow in
harmony with the principles underlying all life. Nature
then must be your study. Never allow authority to be
your teacher, but place it where it belongs, as a finger-post
showing short-cuts to knowledge. The only teacher for

real knowledge is observation or experience. Nor should you overlook the fact that the works of man are as much a part of nature as is the mountain or forest. The city is as much the result of natural laws, as is the burrow of the squirrel or the populous hill of the industrious ant.

Everything on the earth is subject to natural law, and is the result of natural action. All progress must be according to natural laws, and nothing can be accomplished beyond the limitations set by our environment. "The action of environment is the primordial factor of organic evolution."

Nevertheless, our own constitutions and powers may change, nay, must change; and the impossible of to-day will become the commonplace of to-morrow.

It is by a careful study of nature that we can best guide ourselves to progress. For by such knowledge we will not be so inconsequent in throwing ourselves into a contest for which we are in no way prepared, but for which, by care, we may be ready in our descendants in the future.

A regular recurring day of relief from routine, either by rest or recreation, has been a feature in the plan of every religious legislator. In this Moses was preceded and has been followed. Let no inducement lead you to abandon a day of rest. It is at such times that the mind and nervous powers, freed from the drain of routine work, may be directed in reflection to improvement.

The races with a day of rest have without an exception a superior position in every way to those with none. In nothing is this more noticeable than in industrial life, where one would think the loss of a day's work in seven would be felt. Industrially, the rest-day keepers almost in proportion to the strictness of their rest surpass non-resting or partial-resting competitors. For the product and advance of society, and above all for the individual human being, it will be of advantage to adhere to a day of rest.

It will not be wise to cast aside too lightly the customs of society. In dress, for instance, there is a revolt among reasonable persons against the fashions of women's clothing, which renders them incapable of the same physical activity as men. I sympathize with the proposed reform. In thinking over this subject, however, it occurs to me that there may be some philosophy in their fashions. In the least civilized, speaking generally, there is the least drawback in dress to women's activity, and in the most civilized the greatest. High-heeled shoes, corsets, long skirts, unmanageable hats, veils, etc., are from an artistic point of view rarely beautifiers. The pinched feet of high society Chinese women are certainly not pretty. These inventions are those of civilized or semi-civilized man, not of savages.

From some points of view these dress fashions are not favorable to childbearing, but from others they are distinctly so. All these limiting fashions tend to keep women out of the contest of industrial life, and consequently confine them to home or at least to social life.

Home life is conducive to childbearing, while industrial life outside of the home is to women a discourager to childbearing.

The improvement in the condition of women, brought by civilization, has had a constant effect to diminish child-bearing, tending to the extermination of the most civilized. Whether the fashions of dress, etc., have any philosophical basis in counteracting this influence is a matter worthy of thought and study. Fashions in dress come and go. Some of them are said to have had a distinct object in their origin. Large hoops, for instance, it is claimed were devised to secure the virtue of the court ladies of France. It is, however, also said that a certain duchess devised them to conceal a conception not legitimately come by.

While reforms in the line of woman's health, such as abolition of tight lacing, high-heeled shoes, etc., are to be commended, radical and sudden changes should not be lightly undertaken. Before women can be completely emancipated from the limitations under which they now live, with safety to the reproduction of the best, they must consider reproduction the highest and grandest point to which they can attain, and be ready to sacrifice everything to achieve this glory. This is not now the case.

In the ordinary social life certain things are done that are directly disadvantageous, to gain advantage in another direction that will more than counterbalance the first loss. As an illustration of this point we may mention the uniform of soldiers. These are rarely without more or less tinsel. Cumbersome hats like those of the grenadiers of the guard, uncomfortable coats, epaulettes, ornaments, and unstable colors, cuirasses, helmets, etc. ; all these are detriments to the soldier in his soldier's work of campaigning and killing. But the disadvantage of these is much more than counterbalanced by the interest and pride of the soldier in the pomp and glory of his uniform. Thus men are more easily induced to follow the life of' a soldier.

There is, by the way, no occupation so likely to leave one's faculties unused, and therefore to injure what faculties we have and to prevent progress, as the life of a soldier in peace. Avoid it ; but while doing so do not go too far. It will be some time yet before the individual or family can hope to hold what he or it is incapable of defending. So also will it be with nations. Some preparation and training for defence is very essential. In this connection a good maxim may guide you : " The best defence is attack." That is, when it becomes evident that you must fight, make the fighting yourself and make it hot.

Wise courage is the prudent guide by the best road to safety. Wise fear is the same. True cowardice is the avoidance of present evils to encounter more grievous ones later. Prudence will often demand from the far-seeing what to the to-day-man will seem rash risking. Audacity is often the highest prudence. As a general rule what the world calls cowardice is the most imprudent course to follow.

In a charge, for instance, it is usually safer to go clear

through into the enemies' works than to go half way and then turn back. It is harder to hit an armed man rushing toward you than to shoot him when running away. If a soldier shirks his duty altogether he is likely to be shot for desertion ; consequently courage as a rule exposes the individual soldier to the least risks. Society's standard for courage is, of course, derived from its own interest and not that of the individual. It is, therefore, not a complete guide for the safest conduct. Society's necessities, however, oblige it to punish self safe-seeking to the injury of the body politic. Where the natural punishment of society's standard of cowardice is not sufficient, society sets up an artificial punishment to protect itself, and to harmonize individual self-interest with the interest of society.

Life itself is a contest. It is the contest that forces the use and improvement of our faculties.

One of the things to remember is to work and keep your own counsel. Talk if you will, but tell nothing. What is better is to *do* and let others talk. In trouble remember the French maxim, " When the criminal speaks the prosecution is instructed," or another, " He who excuses himself accuses himself."

Man is yet dazzled by show, but he is attracted and awed by mystery. Therefore the silent, about whose plans no one is informed, command attention and respect when a full confession of their schemes would only have let loose criticism and excited resistance. In another old maxim, speech is compared to silver, but silence

to gold. When talking, one's powers are used in enunci-
ation and one's attention is largely fixed on maintaining
one's own argument connected. Therefore a talker can
observe less of what is taking place about him than the
silent. The silent man can be on the watch for characters, tendencies, sympathies, prejudices, etc. in others,
which he can use to his own ends. His silence gives
power. Talk in quantity is sometimes good, but as a rule
it excites argument and resistance. When we would con-
vince or convert others, the true policy is to suggest the
idea for them to follow, rather than to attempt to carry
their conversion in our own minds and by our own trains
of thought. In other words, let them convert themselves
or at least think that they convert themselves. For this
policy few words are necessary. A fact to-day, a hint to-
morrow, and often before you know it you will have a
disciple to out-Herod Herod.

You must always remember that self-interest is the
great mover of mankind. When men serve you their interest must be served. A great politician under our corrupt system needs workers. The successful in this line
secure their agents by making it plainly to their interest
to do the political work. This means corruption. While
politics are corrupt you should never make a business of
them. Many large views are obtained in and through public office. Responsibility and largeness of duty ought to
improve the mental faculties ; but, on the other hand, the
deterioration that ever attends dishonesty must more than
counterbalance any gain of this kind. It is almost im-

possible to-day to do anything in politics without corruption. If a man is not personally dishonest in politics he
must derive advantage from the dishonesty of others.

The progressive degradation of politics in America
doubtless explains the progressive weakening of our public men. In a crisis like the Civil War, those who went
to the front were able to secure political preferment by
merit in public affairs, and not as much as now by combinations, caucuses, and corruptions ; consequently their
characters were not completely contaminated. A total
abstinence from public affairs is not wise nor advantageous. The sensible course is not to make politics, as now
constituted, one's business and means of livelihood, nor
ever to go into the dirty work so common in its activities.

In any effort at reform, such as doing away with
political bosses, remember that it is not oversetting the
man so much as the method that reform will give results
through.

The more recent advance of mankind has probably
been confined to the north temperate and semi-tropic
zones. From our own knowledge of savages and barbarians, from history and from ancient monuments and tradi-
tion in these climates, we may affirm with some show of
accuracy that man in the temperate zone was first a hunter
or savage, then a herdsman or barbarian, and last an
agriculturist making possible extensive manufacture and
commerce. The government best suited to these conditions varies. The qualities necessary to achieve success
as a savage are not those essential to do this in a civilized

man. The savage orator and audacious fighter holds his tribe as their political chief, while the same result is best achieved by us through plots and caucuses, money and workers, and by lying and cheating.

Self-restraint is a very valuable thing. To hold back from present gratification of pleasure or passion, to avert future ills or to gain a future benefit is a quality of greatness. A present sacrifice of pleasure, if practised with judgment, should bring a great future store of enjoyment or avert a great future store of pain. The application of time to labor, rather than to what is called pleasure, is of this class. Man thus obtains capital and position with which to maintain and rear his family. Restraint from illicit sexual intercourse is of great good. Dignity and purity are maintained, and the forces held for the joy of love and reproduction. The question often is, Will you take 10 per cent. from your pleasure of to-day for 90 per cent. of your pleasure in the future ? Or not doing so, cause natural effects to take 90 per cent. from your future pleasure to allow yourself 10 per cent. to-day.

Self-restraint is one of the essentials, but it may be carried to excess, as we see in misers.

What is called pleasure as a pursuit has a monotony and an absence of sound object that defeats itself. Thus we find that the most unhappy and miserable people are those *blasé* by a continuous pursuit of pleasure. *Blasé* people are never found amongst the industrious. While all work and no play makes Jack a dull boy, so all play and no work makes John a worthless man. All play and no work has but one end as regards pleasure, and that is its destruction.

One of the so-called pursuits of pleasure practised by perverse persons is illicit sexual intercourse. Even if disease does not come, this defeats itself. This intercourse without love is a very inferior exhibition of lust. It is true that the mere act of reproduction has by nature a pleasure for man, but this act practised with prostitutes is followed by a disgust that to a great degree neutralizes the animal pleasure of the act. If a man descends at all to illicit intercourse, it must be largely, at least, confined to prostitutes. It is a curious medical fact that more venereal disease is contracted from disgraced women, not regularly so known, than from professional prostitutes.

Association with a kept woman or mistress is a particularly perilous form for illicit intercourse to take. If she be taken a virgin and acquire your love and respect to the point of inducing marriage, she would as a wife bear a cloud on her reputation that society would not forgive ; and she, you, and the children born would all feel it. A mistress may take a hold on the affections which will discourage marriage or cause it to come late, if at all. A mistress may come to love her master, which is an exceedingly unpleasant situation. Such a woman is capable of ruining a man's life.

Alphonse Daudet wrote a book, *Sappho*, dedicated to his son, to warn him from this very danger. It is much greater than one might at first sight think. I know of several instances where mistresses, discarded for wives,

10

have wrecked families. There are cases on record where the mistress has even shot down and killed the man.

Life with a mistress is a revolt against one of the foundations of society "marriage," and cannot be tolerated by society in a sound condition. Therefore the *liaison* must be kept secret.

In the heat of passion the Devil may not seem such a bad fellow as he is painted. But to live with him in cold storage, at your elbow, cheek by jowl, during your sober moments, is a folly.

> " The Devil in sport 's a gay partie ;
> The Devil in thought 's a cactus-tree."

The Devil is at home in heat. It is a good man's passion that makes him friendly with the fiend, and the fiend is lively in his passion's fires ; but the passion gone, cold thought comes in. The Devil cannot be gay in such chilly company, and the Devil either leaves or makes a very uncomfortable and disagreeable third party very much *de trop*.

To be loved by a mistress is to have the fate of Prometheus. To love a mistress is to wear the ears of an ass if not the horns of the French. The chapter on Family Government contains some further points on this subject.

Love is the spiritualized instinct of reproduction. As I have already said, its God amongst the Greeks was Cupid, the child. The object of love, as implanted in us by nature, is the child. This is its fruit. It cannot long exist without the child. The world continually applies the word love to states of feelings that are really lust, friendship, affection, esteem, or something else, but not love.

Love is something mysterious and beautiful. In its perfection it is beyond compare. The animal passions which form its basis should by no means be allowed to drag love's beauties, mysteries, and grandeurs into the mire of mere lust.

How easy restraint in these matters can be made, may be seen by the fact that our education, excluding married women and men from love by the still single, prevents their being sexually loved by the single.

In a healthy society such unholy love is very rarely seen. The education prevents the aberration. Without the education certainly there is no way to explain why the single should not be as likely to love the married as to love other single persons.

Love flies with the heart at first from maid to maid and at last in the fire of passion fuses another heart to yours. With some there is at first an uncertainty of choice ; therefore, a little maxim is commended to keep you out of trouble—" Talk love, never write it."

Men should marry and women should marry. It is in the child, the natural bond, that their instincts and passions achieve glory. But the first intuitive excursions of love may well be diplomatically left non-committal.

Woman is like the sapphire, beautiful indeed, but to be fully appreciated she must have the man as the sapphire needs the diamond, that hard and brilliant gem, to show its attractions. These two gems, generally so excellent together, do not always constitute a good combination. Their sizes, colors, and adaptabilities must be harmonious to make a successful and beautiful jewel. So it is with men and women. Each individual may be admirable, but still not capable of making a happy union with an admirable individual of the opposite sex. The casual throwing together of men and women in matrimony is no evidence of a correct combination for the creation of the child.

It is a kindly rule to attribute to mankind the best motives by which they might have been actuated in their doings. The reverse, however, is the common and uncomfortable practice. All men have some imperfections ; there is consequently a fellow-feeling amongst us for errors. One, therefore, who looks for others' defects and pulls them into the light, though applauded by our jealousies, can never be popular.

The weakness of mankind, however, makes caution in all human dealings a necessity. Every man has some angel and some devil in him. Look for the angel but guard against the devil.

In common business intercourse there are many little things of value to an observer as indications of character. The man with the diamond-pin will usually be of a speculative disposition. He who is exact and punctual in all engagements is usually conservative and honest. The liar in small things, and he who steals others' time in lack of punctuality, is rarely reliable. The observation of such every-day traits of character may be made a useful measure for larger things. It is indeed curious how much of a person's qualities may be discovered by his face, dress, or habits. Thus far our judgment of individuals from such sources has been more a matter of instinct than of reason. Likes and dislikes at first sight are felt even by very young children. These instinctive attractions or repulsions extend to the intercourse of man with animals and of animals with man.

Such impulses derived from the inherited experience of the race should never be neglected. On the other hand, it should be remembered that a natural repulsion, reliable as against the probability of pleasant personal intercourse, or an attraction guiding us accurately to a sympathetic nature, may, in neither case, be 'an index to the useful or undesirable qualities favorable or unfavorable in a servant or an agent. An old saw says, "The man whom the town dogs follow is naught." This may be remembered in figuring up the value of social qualities in business affairs.

It is a good rule to follow first impressions in dealing with mankind. But a clear and catholic view of our means and aims should guide this remarkable instinct. Unconscious cerebration is a certain element in brain-activity. We lose a name and cannot recall it by the will, but by and by, when we are thinking of something else, it comes back to us. The intuitions are something of this nature. As we say, we feel things are thus and so ; we take a prejudice for or against a person, but we cannot formulate a reason.

It seems strange that though man in phrenology, palmistry, etc., has so often tried to formulate these feelings, so well recognized, into a reliable science, he has thus far failed in securing the approval of the judicious.

The changed condition under which men live, compared to those of a few thousand years ago, should be deemed a sufficient cause to make us question carefully a first prejudice for or against a person. Qualities, good or bad, for a former condition, the opinion of which we inherit in an instinct, may be of different social effect at this time.

It has been frequently said that genius is kin to insanity. It is a saying altogether untrue. A man who sees too far ahead of his contemporaries to be understood is generally accused by their stupidity with craziness, but his genius in so perceiving the truer and higher relation of things is not the result of a defect of mind, but of a superiority of mind. So, also in other manifestations of genius.

The over-use of the highest intellectual qualities, like their insufficient use, may disease or destroy the brain medium of their manifestations as in Swift, Pascal, and in other remembered men. Genius, in itself, however, can have no possible kinship with insanity.

Insanity is a paralysis of the highest brain functions, and is indicated not by any high mental manifestations, but by the uncontrollable or ill co-ordinated activities of lower brain centres. Insanity is a disease of the highest brain tissue and debilitates if it does not destroy its powers. It is of exactly the same character of paralysis that we see in the motor centres situated in the lower spinal column when locomotor ataxia appears. In this disease, this nervous centre is attacked and its progressive paralysis is shown in the progressive loss of motion and control of motion in the legs, not by a superiority of motion anywhere.

If one desires to be a stranger to imagination in others, there is no place so certain to realize this desire as an insane asylum. The poverty of thought in the hospitals of the unfortunate, whose higher qualities have gone leaving the lower ones without a head, is striking to one expecting to find in them some confirmation of the popular saying.

Genius should be sought. Insanity should be avoided. The searcher may rest assured that, while he may find geniuses who have become insane, he will never find genius in the insane.

One of our customs that is most often decried is the indulgence of gossip. It is generally spoken of as wholly bad. The truth is, however, that it is of great value. The decrease of gossip in this country is really a cause of alarm. Gossip is the executioner of the unwritten, social law. Many a man and women is kept in the traces by the fear of what people will say. Other reasons hold them, but this is the most potent to keep them good. This, of course, is only true when the standard of society is correct.

Social rules have been evolved from man's experience

and are for the benefit of humanity. They change according to his needs. To openly violate a social tenet
will make the individual uncomfortable, at least. Consequently such rules should be observed. The fashion
now is to denounce large families. Such a fatal aberration of course must not be bowed to. This fashion became prevalent in the Sandwich Islands. Under it the
native population has decreased from 400,000 to less than
20,000 in seventy or eighty years. It is true that the
vices and diseases of the civilized are exceedingly fatal
to most savages. Smallpox, for instance, in 1853, the
first year of its introduction to Honolulu, destroyed one
half the native population ; but, besides this, savages in
contact with the civilized seem incapable or unwilling to
breed.

As an Indian Commissioner I have observed the fact
that those Indians near the white settlements lose their
reproductive power as compared to those farther removed
from this influence.

For instance, in two Indian villages of Southern Cali-.
fornia, Sequan and Los Coyotes, there is in each nearly
the same population, between eighty and ninety. The
first is near the city of San Diego, and subject to the influences of civilization. There were in this place in my
last visit only eight children and no babies. Los Coyotes
is on the desert side of the Sierra, far from any white settlement or route of travel. There were at the same time
thirty-four children at this settlement. Whether fashion
or disease is the main cause of these diminished popula-

tions, the extermination that has overtaken the Tasmanian and so many of the American tribes awaits them. So also it awaits us if this fashion prevail. We must avoid this rock.

The destruction of these isolated and sometimes Arcadian populations on their contact with our cruel civilization shows us something else. It is that it will not do to attempt an escape from plain present evils by going out of the movement of the world. If whole populations have been swept away in a few years, owing to their not being inured to the hardships and dangers of civilization, we must anticipate a similar fate in the future for populations similarily situated. Consequently, distant islands or secluded valleys are contra-indicated for homes.

No thought is better, no effort more useful than that which seeks to find how to perpetuate and improve life in reproduction.

The motive for good deeds furnished by the religious legislators of the past was a part and interest in eternity.

No motive can be greater. The things of this world must indeed seem paltry in contrast to such an expectation.

Let us then seize upon this motive. Let us prove its reality and possibility, and let our aims be to keep forever lighted the sacred fires of life that burn in our existence. This we can do in our children.

A part in eternity is made possible by procreation. The Child then is our Future. It should be our Religion.

DIET.

L IFE in man involves a continuous waste and wear in the vital machinery, and requires for its manifestation a supply of fuel or aliment. The restricted capacity of the human being as to aliment-storage requires, as an absolute essential to life, a frequent renewal of supply. In practice we find it best to make this renewal from twice to three times in the twenty-four hours.

The word diet as used in this chapter is understood to mean all things taken by man to provide energy, and to replace, retard, or accelerate waste, and the manner of taking these.

Diet in its completeness comprises what we eat in foods, what we drink in fluids, what we breathe in the air, and what we use in narcotics, stimulants, or drugs.

The best diet varies with age, idiosyncrasy, occupation, health, and with climate. Thus in age :—The food of the babe is properly confined to milk. For the strong man this food is too dilute and bulky to be a complete diet. So the food of the adult with teeth and a completed digestive apparatus is altogether unsuited to the babe without teeth, and with a small stomach and simple organs of assimilation. With old age and the loss of teeth and digestive vigor and lessened capacity for labor, the foods of the child may again become appropriate.

Thus in idiosyncrasy :—In general, fish form a good element in diet ; still with some they produce indigestion or marked constitutional disturbance. Strawberries, usually agreeable and easy of disposition by the internal economy, with some produce a rash. Milk, generally acceptable at all ages, and in its constituents a perfect food, with some produces indigestion so marked as to make it unavailable as an article of diet. Apples, an excellent fruit for most, produce in some disorders which I have even known to go to the extent of causing temporary diabetes whenever this food was eaten.

Eggs are almost universally friendly to the system, and are a perfect food as to all the necessary constituents ; still they cause serious trouble to some persons when eaten, even convulsions occasionally resulting from their ingestion. I have a case of this kind in one of my children. He can eat no eggs nor anything containing them without distress, and has had this peculiarity from the first time he took them.

On the other hand, foods and combinations of food generally disadvantageous, such as lobsters and milk or cherries and milk, etc., seem to have no bad effects on some people.

Thus, in occupations, a full diet of coarse food will be not only appropriate, but as to its fulness, essential to the health and activity of a physical worker in the open air. To the same person in a sedentary pursuit such a

diet would cause inconvenience, doubtless to be followed
by ill health. The brain worker needs as liberal a support
as does the muscle worker, but it is of a different kind.
The economy of cookery, that is, the partial digestion of
food by the chemistry of cooking, outside of the body, is
particularly advantageous to the brain worker.

Thus in health a diet may be good or bad, according
to one's condition. A person in perfect health has, as a
rule, a pretty wide dietary margin ; still an invalid's diet
of soft and simple foods frequently given, is quite inappropriate for the whilom invalid when well. So also
the mixed strong diet of the healthy is bad for the
invalid. The well man requires concentrated food in
sufficient quantity to obviate the necessity of a feeding so
frequent as to interfere with labor. The well man's diet
probably should also be of a character to require a certain
energy in the digestive organs.

The invalid, on the other hand, requires less food, for
if properly treated he will be in repose. His energies
also should be given the fullest play to repair the ravages
of his illness and to drive off disease, and should therefore be spared from all unnecessary digestive work.
Drugs enter the diet of invalids for special purposes,
often to kill or to deaden specific germs. Their effects
on the normal man are frequently bad.

Thus a diet containing considerable arsenic may be
advantageous to one suffering with eczema, while to a
well person such a diet would probably produce some
form of skin trouble, or at least digestive disturbance.

In Styria this drug is more customarily consumed than in other portions of the world. Many general conditions of the population of that district would indicate that its effects are physically bad. The mothers, for instance, are noticeably lacking in lactation.

A diet with mercury or iodide of potassium is thought essential for one suffering with that dreadful disease, "syphilis." Certainly the destructive effects of these drugs on the healthy would make them ill advised as a general addition to the diet. Iodide of potassium produces serious irruptions when used in excess, and the effects of mercury are too well known to require mention.

Hospital records indicate, and certain physicians, friends of mine, estimate the proportion of the population in American cities more or less tainted with syphilis to be very considerable. It is thus seen that mercury and iodide of potassium are or ought to be quite important articles of diet. As an indication of what this taint may be, we may take the figures of the English army which show a proportion of one in three treated annually for venereal disease, or, to be exact, 329 cases in the 1,000. These were of course due to all the different sorts of venereal diseases.

Quinine makes a good addition to the diet of a malarian, but the effects of this drug on the digestion and nervous system contraindicate it for the healthy.

Cod-liver oil has been the best addition ever made to the diet of consumptives, and of those suffering from some other similar wasting diseases. It is also good in many bad constitutional conditions, for instance, eczema. But in large quantities, such as would be suitable to tolerance in this class of invalids, this food would be disadvantageous to the healthy, as encouraging too much the formation of useless adipose.

Thus in climate, the fruits of the tropics, with such grain additions as rice or sago, would be fatal in the arctic zone as a diet, for it would provide insufficient calorific to resist the cold. On the other hand, the blubber food of the Esquimaux would be equally inappropriate at the equator. A long-continued use of the foods of the tropics, or the diet of the Icy Circle, renders man incapable of modifying his digestive apparatus to the use of the dietary extreme opposite his own. Thus an Esquimaux cannot live long at the equator, nor can an African native live long near the poles.

In a less degree the most appropriate diets for varying climatic conditions differ everywhere. The importance of a careful study of foods and of conditions will be more readily perceived, perhaps, when we remember the diseases due entirely to vicious and improper diet.

The pellegra is a disease general amongst the poor people of the valley of the river Po in Italy. The misery and distress this disease causes in the population is great. It has its origin in the diet of the country, which is largely composed of maize or corn. This is eaten generally in a condition somewhat fermented or spoiled.

The scurvy, a malady most frequent formerly at sea, but now happily but little known, committed at one time fearful ravages. Whole ships' crews were disabled by it; whole ships' crews occasionally died of it. Scarcely ever was a voyage of any duration made without a consider-able visitation of scurvy to the crew. Armies like that of St. Louis in Egypt perished of it. Scurvy is a dietary disease due largely to the continued absence of vegetables, or fruit acids from the foods used. This discovery of the fact did away with its dangers.

Recent voyages in the arctic show some curious things in relation to scurvy. Lemon juice, for instance, it has been found, is not so good a preventative as a moderate amount of alcohol. In two ships in the same expedition, one using lemon juice and the other beer, scurvy appeared in the first ship and could not be eradicated, while it did not occur at all in the beer-using crew.

It is now certain that beer, wine, and spirits are a better preventative in the arctic against scurvy than lime juice, which was the agent heretofore used for this purpose.

Ergotism is a disease prevalent in parts of Germany. It is due to a parasite of the rye. This grain is there the one most used.

Leprosy is another dreadful disease partly perhaps attributable to diet. It has been suffered and misunderstood in all climates and in all quarters of the world. Its original cause is said to be the use of stale or spoiled fish, continuously and in considerable quantity, as food.

Many other diseases more or less due to diet might be cited, but it is as well to rest with these certainties. With this information further looked into no family can

be careless about its diet. The cases of poisoning from
canned goods, from ice-cream, from spoiled or adulterated
foods are the underlinings only to keep one's attention
on this important question.

The marked effect of foods upon birds and animals
is indicated by their flavor. The sage-hen of Utah is
exceedingly sweet and delicate to the taste, in the spring ;
in the fall, on the contrary, it has a rank flavor of sage,
due to its feeding at this time principally on this food.
The canvas-back ducks that visit the Chesapeake Bay are
deemed by epicures to be the best for the table. Their
flavor is attributed to the wild celery upon which they
there feed. These flavors in the flesh seem always influenced by diet. The same influences may be seen in
the secretions of animals. The milk of cows changes
perceptibly in color, specific gravity, flavor, and composition with changes of diet. Hay alone will make the
milk specially white and poor in cream ; alfalfa will make
it watery, with a peculiar and not over-pleasant flavor.
Carrots in quantity will give a rich color and more cream,
etc., etc.

Whether effects are produced by foods on the brain
similar to those on the muscles, endurance, and flavor of
flesh has not been demonstrated. The popular belief in
favor of this opinion should be presumed to have some
foundation until the contrary is proved, for the analogy
is too strong to be passed by. Even vegetables and
fruits of identical varieties vary in flavor in a marked
manner in different climates and soils, that is, with differ-

ent plant foods and conditions. Apples in the North are good, in the South poor ; peaches on heavy, wet soils are indifferent, while on warm, light ones they reach excellence ; while for the pear the conditions are reversed. The effect of very slight differences are notorious in grapes, through the flavor of the wine made from them.

Fanatics and empirical reformers every now and then establish some dietary regulation as a part of their creeds or forms. Sometimes their rules are based on very sensible observations. The code of Moses and of the Talmud is particularly worthy of study. Some animals, as the pig and rabbit, are especially subject to parasites which, as in the case of trichinæ, when introduced into man are dangerous. The meat of such animals should be well cooked, with a view to destroying its dangers, and I believe also should be as a rule avoided. In some countries, as a few years ago in Cyprus, all animals seemed to be more or less infected with parasites, and several of my friends contracted parasites in that island as they thought from eating ill-cooked meat, the meat coming from the cattle of the country.

The prohibition of certain animals for eating by the early religious legislators sometimes grew out of the custom of having certain animals sacred to the tribe. Consequently we cannot give too much attention to old dietaries, for these were often made not upon scientific reason, but upon reasons totally disconnected with dietary advantages.

The ideas and codes of religious sects in regard to food

11

and feeding should not be despised. The observance of feasts and fasts has sound reason for it. To astonish one's stomach occasionally with a large meal of a different make-up from the ordinary is usually beneficial ; so also is a reasonable and occasional fast or abstinence, especially in the spring of the year. Pregnant women, however, are excepted. A regular life and a regular diet is good, but it should be tempered by a little judicious irregularity to be best.

Of course all such schemes as the exclusion of meat or animal food, or the exclusion of the science of cooking from the preparation of food, etc., are not to be thought of. Such ideas are the follies of the extremist. The impossible Hindoo will eat nothing that has been deprived of life. He tells you this while he crushes between his teeth the life germ of the rice seed, and while he munches a vegetable torn from the ground and dead. Man is a predatory, omnivorous animal. His life is accompanied always by the destruction of other life, amount- · ing daily to a great figure. Hindoo ideas are consequently not now practical.

I once visited a colony whose rules were founded on a so-called spiritual revelation. In these rules all animal or cooked food was excluded from the diet. Milk, butter, cheese, eggs, and all meats or products of animals were forbidden. So also were all vegetables, such as potatoes, which cannot be eaten raw. I took dinner with them. The meal consisted of walnuts, dried apples, raw peanuts, and raisins. One member of the colony, its chief, seemed to thrive, but the rest were weak and ethereal in appearance, and incapable of prolonged energetic work.

The progress of man is not likely to make it advantageous to give more time and energy to digestion than now. This would be the case were an exclusive vegetable diet adopted. The size of the stomach, jaw, teeth, etc., is diminishing in the civilized man. It is therefore plain on this account alone that the food of the civilized must be more concentrated and more regularly taken than is essential with the savage. A caution seems appropriate in this connection. In our progressive change toward more concentrated food, we should expect the nerves giving notice that a sufficient quantity of food has been taken, to be often deceived by the difference in bulk and quick consumption of civilized diet, and should consequently avoid the danger of overeating.

The tendency in diet has been toward concentrated food, easily and promptly digested. This food judiciously chosen is the best, for it gives liberty to the greatest amount of energy for other achievement besides digestion. The cow eating bulky aliment, which to be digested, requires to be chewed, and chewed again in the cud, passes its waking hours on its food supply and assimilation. Such an animal is incapable of greatness. The digestive organs of the horse require a certain amount of bulk to work well. In the domestication of this animal the efforts of man have been to concentrate the food used as much as is consistent with its organs of assimilation, and thus to apply the energies of the horse to work rather than to digestion. A horse put out to grass without work will gain in size, especially the stomach, and fall off in energy : with work on a grass diet, he will fall off both in weight and energy.

In all diets the machinery and mechanism of the digestion, as well as the capacity of the organs themselves, must be considered ; consequently a grass diet can never be good for man, because his stomach and vital organs are unsuited to such food. So equally a meat diet would not do for a cow.

As the egg is the common source of life in all mammals, so milk is the common food of the young of all, and the milk of one is available for any. Still the milk varies, human milk having most sugar.

As the lines of development diverge, so the food changes ; thus we may presume that further evolution of man will involve further change of food. In fact, a careful examination indicates a tendency to perform digestive and masticating work outside the body, also an equally clear tendency toward concentrated forms of nourishment, leading often to pure stimulation by such high concentrations as we find in alcohol. The increase of butter and sugar consumption is in the same line. All the CHO compounds are stimulating. Inasmuch as the evolution of the digestive organs to meet necessary requirements for a higher life-organization would be arrested if diet remained uuchanged, we must perceive that persistance in the *statu quo* of diet involves stagnation in other lines. Thus, while such a diet would avoid the loss of many individuals and of more or less discomfort and danger in nearly all, it would also eliminate such individuals in their descendants from the race progress, and eventuate in extermination.

Radical conservatism in diet is neither scientific nor safe.

If we are to have further progress in the human race, it is to be presumed that the diet will be much modified, and consequently the digestive organs modified also to meet new requirements. We have something of this kind in the loss of function of the appendix vermiformis.

All this would doubtless be in the line of economy in time and energy in supplying the system with food.

Consequently a race or family not progressing in this way, would soon be fatally handicapped in the life struggle and progress of humanity. A diet thoroughly in harmony with our present digestive organs is not from that fact a good one. It may be good for the individual.

From present indications we can judge little of the future. It may be that we will come to a point where the alimentary substances will be taken from the ground by chemical process, without the intervention of plants and animals. We may also come to a point where the entire preparatory work will be done outside of the body, in which case we may take a hypodermic injection for a dinner, and become independent of mouth, teeth, stomach, and intestines.

We may consider this possibility exceedingly remote, but we should never lose sight of the modifications that

have occurred in our diet and in our digestive tract, nor
of the probable continuation of these modifications toward
a more economical method of supplying our vital needs.

As far as our digestive organs at their present stage of
evolution are concerned, it has been ascertained with
sufficient accuracy for all intents and purposes, what
character and quantity of food is required for men in the
temperate zone. We have prison diets, soldiers' diets,
sailors' diets, etc., now arranged on a scientific basis in
place of the old empirical one.

Yeo's table for the adult is :

Albuminous foods....................	100 grammes.
Fats................................	90 "
Starch	300 "
Salts..............................	30 "
Water..............................	2,800 "

Foster and Voit's table is :

Albuminoids.........................	118 grammes.
Carbohydrates...	392.3 "
Fats................................	88.4 "

In these foods there is of nitrogen 18.3 grammes ; carbon, 328 grammes.

De Chaumont's table for an adult of 150 lbs. weight and
doing an average amount of work is :

Albuminoids.........................	4.5 oz.
Fats................................	3.75 "
Carbohydrates.......................	18.00 "
Salts..	1.12 "

The British soldier's ration is :

Albuminoids	3.86 oz.
Fats	1.30 "
Carbohydrates	17.43 "
Salts	.81 "

This ration is deficient in fats, and the high mortality of British soldiers in garrison may be attributed in part to this error. A considerable part of this excessive mortality is in diseases for which fats are generally prescribed.

The following tables are taken from the *Best Rations for the Soldier*, by Col. Jos. R. Smith, M.D.

By general experience and individual experiment, we have discovered a certain amount of food which will sustain an average individual in good health ; and, also, that much less than this will not suffice, though we do not know that a little less would not suffice. We have discovered, too, that certain combinations and proportions of different foods are best in the larger number of cases.

As large numbers of men are involved in these experiments, the application of " averages " comes to our aid, viz. : That property of the " average," in virtue of which, from a large number of specific cases, every one inaccurate in different directions, an idea may be deduced which is very near, indeed, to accuracy.

I proceed to give the amounts of food necessary to sustain in health and strength an adult male for twenty-four hours, as determined theoretically and (by experience) practically by different parties.

TABLE I.

Amount of Food Required per Man, per Day, as Determined in Actual Trial.

		AVERAGE.	TOTAL SOLID FOOD.	
I.	By Prof. J. C. Dalton.	Fresh meat.............16 ozs. Bread..................19 " Butter or fat........... 3.5 "	38.5 ozs.	For a "man in full health, and taking free exercise in the open air."
2.	Typical Ration of English Army.	Meat....................16 ozs. Bread...................20 " Or biscuit...............16 " Vegetables (fresh)........ 8 " Or vegetables (preserved) ⎱ 2 " or rice or peas........ ⎰ Sugar................... 2 " Tea..................... ⅛ " Coffee .... ⅓ " Salt.................... ⅔ " Pepper............... ¹⁄₃₆ " Lime-juice ⎰ when fresh ⎱ 1 " ⎱ vegetables ⎰ ⎰ are not issued ⎱ Rum.................... ¼ gill	Max. 46 ozs. to min. 36 ozs.	Lime-juice at discretion of the General Officer Commanding, on the recommendation of the Medical Officer.
3.	Italian Army. Type B.	Bread............ ......32.378 ozs. Meat, fresh......... 5.291 " Bacon........ ..... .529 Pastry (macaroni, etc.) 7.054 " Vegetables.......... 1.763 " Salt and pepper...... .7054 "	47.015 ozs.	In Nos. 3 and 4, wine, 25 centiliters; coffee, 15 grammes(over ¼ oz.), and sugar, 22 grammes(over ¾ oz.), should be added, being allowed

		AVERAGE.	TOTAL SOLID FOOD.	
4.	Italian Army. Type E.	Corn-meal........... ....24.689 ozs. Meat, fresh........... 5.291 " Bacon................ .529 " Vegetables............. 2.645 " Cheese............. 1.164 " Salt and pepper....... 1.411 "	34.318 ozs.	
5.	Ration of the Army of the United States of North America	Pork or bacon..........12 ozs. Or fresh beef or mutton. 20 " Or salt beef............22 " Soft bread or flour......18 " Or hard bread..........16 " Or corn-meal..........20 " Beans or peas.......... 2.4 " Or rice or hominy....... 1.6 " Coffee, green.......... . 1.6 " Or coffee, roasted and } 1.28 " ground........... } Or tea................. .32 " Sugar................. 2.4 " Vinegar.............. .32 gills Salt................... .64 ozs. Pepper............... .04 "	Max. 48.6 ozs. to min. 32 ozs.	
6.	Rations of the Navy of the United States of North America	No. 1. { Salt pork.... ......18 ozs. Beans or peas..... 7.5 " Biscuit............14 " Tea............. ....½ " Sugar............. 4 " Pickles .... 1.14 " Molasses.......... 1.57 " Vinegar.......... ½ pint No. 2. { Salt beef..........16 ozs. Flour............. 8 " Dried fruit..... .. 2 " Biscuit, tea, sugar, pickles, molasses, and vinegar, the same as in Ration 1.		

		AVERAGE.	TOTAL SOLID FOOD.	
No. 3.	{	Preserved meat....12 ozs. Rice.............. 8 " Butter.......... ... 2 " Dessicated mixed } vegetables .... } 1 " Biscuit, tea, sugar, pickles, molasses, and vinegar, as in Ration 1.	Max. 48 ozs. to min. 38 ozs.	
No. 4.	{	Preserved meat....12 " Butter........... 2 " Dessicated tomatoes 6 " Biscuit, tea, sugar, pickles, molasses, and vinegar, as in Ration 1.		

In the above rations, fresh meat,
20 ozs., or preserved meat, 12
ozs., may be substituted for the
ration of salt pork or beef.
Soft bread or flour, 16 ozs., may
be substituted for biscuit.
Coffee, 2 ozs., or cocoa, 2 ozs.,
may be substituted for tea ; rice,
or beans, 8 ozs., may be substituted for each other.   Vegetables of equal value may be
substituted for beans or peas in
No. 1, and for flour and dried
fruits in No. 2.
Canned vegetables, 6 ozs., may be
substituted for dessicated vegetables in No. 3.
Canned tomatoes, 6 ozs., may be
substituted for dessicated in
No. 4.

The foregoing amounts of food are in avoirdupois
ounces, and have undergone the test of experience.

Concerning the first, Dalton, in his work on physiology says: " From experiments performed while living on an exclusive diet of bread, fresh meat, and butter, with coffee and water for drink, we have found that the entire quantity of food required during twenty-four hours, by a man in full health and taking free exercise in open air, is as follows: Meat, 16 ozs.; bread, 19 ozs.; butter or fat, 3½ ozs.; water, 52 fluid ozs."

The second, third, and fourth rations are those of the British and Italian armies. I have given these, because my knowledge concerning them is precise and definite. The amounts of food are authoritative, the figures having been furnished by the authorities in Rome and London to the United States ministers resident in those cities, and by them transmitted to the State Department in Washington.

Accompanying Number 2, came the following: " On active service abroad, in the field, the ration is fixed according to the exigencies in each case, but the following scale is laid down as a guide."

The Italian authorities write, concerning 3 and 4 : " It is established that for the maximum nutrition of soldiers from eighteen to twenty grammes of nitrogen (azote), and from three hundred and ten to three hundred and fifty of carbon are necessary." Six types of rations used were also sent, of which I have presented type B as of the greatest weight, and type E of the least weight.

It must be remembered that all these rations, perhaps appropriate for the climate and places where formulated, can not be so for all climates and places, nor for all digestions. The fact that scurvy, a preventable disease due to diet, is prevalent in nearly all armies and navies, even in peace, shows that these rations are far from perfect, or else that the soldiers do not have the ration the government provides. In the years between 1869 and 1873 it has figured as a disease to the extent of from 6 to 12 % in the Austrian army. It has occurred in our own army. The law permits in this country the company officers to sell a portion of the soldier's ration, and to buy for him whatever they choose. It is a practice to thus sell a certain part of the ration and to apply the money, not to foods, but to what is called a post fund. This fund supports bands, libraries, etc. Such a system must be wrong in principle, and subject to great abuses. In some places the money obtained from the ration is applied to still other purposes, but not for food. At one place this curtailment of the ration resulted in the soldiers receiving 18 ozs. of bread instead of 18 ozs. of flour, equalling a loss of N. 37 grs., and C. 894 grs. Abuses arising from this practice may be the real cause of scurvy in the armies and navies of different countries rather than a really defective ration. (Col. J. B. Smith, M. D.)

Fifty-two fluid ounces of water is by Dalton deemed sufficient for an adult in the temperate zone. This quantity can not be constant, for the amount of water necessary or best for man must vary with the temperature and occupation.

In the above tables the foods spoken of are:

Albuminoids; these are the components of meats, beans, cheese, etc.

Fats; these are fats, butter, oil, etc.

Hydro-carbons; these are sugar and starch, as found in grains, potatoes, etc.

Salts; these are minerals, such as chloride of sodium, common table salt, etc. All of the essentials are found in milk.

The value of different foods in diets depends very much on their preparation. Some foods are most easily assimilated when raw or uncooked, as lettuce, butter, milk, ripe fruits, etc. But the great majority of the articles of food used by man can be partially prepared for assimilation by cooking. Such germs or parasites as they may contain are also destroyed. The energies of man are by this means saved to a considerable extent from the time and work of digestion necessary in other animals without this aid, and the body from some of the dangers of disease.

Cooking, however, is often so badly done that the digestibility of the food treated is impaired, and not improved. It is not possible to enter here upon a treatise on cooking, but we may properly call attention to the fact that the nerves conveying to our nerve centres the sensations of taste are governed largely by the hereditary results of experiment as to the good or bad in foods, and only secondarily and much less reliably by education. Foods, correct in composition but without the flavors

associated with good foods by our nerves of taste, are
not only disagreeable, but fail to secure by reflex stimulation the secretion of saliva, gastric juices, etc., essential
to their proper digestion. Consequently, flavors play an
important part in artificially prepared foods. Foods in
their natural condition confess correctly their appropriateness in diet. Stale lettuce, bad butter, diseased or
spoilt milk, decayed meat, and unripe fruit all tell their
tale at once. Cooked foods that taste badly, if not actually inappropriate for the body in quality, composition,
or chemical condition, are so from their deception of the
nerves of taste, and should be avoided. We may, indeed, educate our tastes, but, unfortunately, their education is as often bad as it is good. Frequently, too,
certain condiments, good in moderation and under
certain conditions, as pepper, spices, curries, etc., are
taken to excess or made to cover defects in cooking that
would otherwise be very apparent.[1]

The chemical changes in foods, under the influence of
heat, time, etc., are great, and should be studied by
every family founder. Butter, for instance, may be
cooked so that it makes the article which it is intended

---

[1] A study of the introduction and use amongst us of the various
condiments is both interesting and instructive. The present almost
universal use of these agents has for its presumable utility the stimulation and hastening of digestion. From this we can perceive the
advantage to man of any saving in time or energy in digestion, for to
the extent of such saving the energies are liberated for other things.
Abuse in the use of condiments is easy to come to under our high
pressure of life, and should be guarded against.

to improve difficult, if not impossible, of digestion ; and so of a number of articles of diet. The preparation of food for the sick or convalescent demands special attention. The rule in this matter is to seek natural foods, such as milk, and to study simplicity in their preparation.

Water is an article which in some form is an absolute essential to man. As a rule the purer it is the better it is. It may be mixed with alcohol, tea, coffee, fruit juices, and more or less adulterated in many ways. Water may be charged naturally with mineral constituents. When the amount of minerals contained is large, especially of some kinds, water becomes unsuited to man's use and may become of no value to him in diet, as is the case with sea water.

Men have fasted for considerable periods. Dr. Tanner and others have been carefully watched in experiments of this kind, and it is now considered established that it is possible for a human being to go for many days without food in the ordinary acceptance of the term. Forty-eight days is probably the longest period during which man has abstained from food and lived, although considerably longer periods have been mentioned. But in no case has man been recorded as going for a lengthened period without some form of water. This fluid is, therefore, the first essential of man after air. Animals, it must be said, however, do seem to go for extraordinary periods without water. In the deserts of California, lizards, rabbits, and other small animals, and in places where no water seems accessible,

ground squirrels, owls, etc., live five or six months and
even longer with no apparent supply of this fluid.
Whether such animals have some means of obtaining
water unknown to us, say from certain plants, or whether
they actually live for long periods without any, I am unable to say. The life of these animals is interesting as
indicating that water is at least not so continuous a necessity to animal life as has been thought.[1] Doubtless
for man to reach such a stage would require many ages
of adaptation. Men vary greatly in respect to their use
of water. I recollect the Bedouin Arabs on the deserts
of Upper Egypt to have been exceedingly abstemious in
their use of water on the march. Apart from the Nile
the water throughout Egypt and the adjacent countries
is scant, and as a rule bad from excess of mineral constituents. The Bedouins are doubtless wise in using this
desert water as little as possible.

The character of the mineral carried in water has a
marked influence on those using it. Some minerals
induce anæmia with its surface-showing of pallor in the
white race, others, as water containing lime, seem to
produce vigor, large frames, and a rosy complexion.
Distilled and rain water are free from any appreciable
mineral, and may therefore be boiled for considerable
periods without danger of increasing the proportion of
mineral through partial evaporation of the water. Good

[1] The sheep in California are not taken to water during the rainy
season, when the food is green. They obtain all the moisture they
need from the grass,

spring, or hard water, is often rendered unfit for use in this way. While an excess of mineral is bad, it is a matter of doubt whether a reasonable amount of mineral in drinking water is not better for man than none at all. The inhabitants of lime stone districts would indicate that this is sometimes the case. The presumption in general should be in favor of the pure water.

Pure rain water, it should be remembered, is especially liable to take up certain minerals, such as lead. Rain water also accumulates, while falling, the germs of certain innocent animalculi, and may accumulate the germs of dangerous ones. The innocent ones are those which have been studied. These multiply with extraordinary rapidity, but apparently exhaust the food in the water, and in about three weeks die off and nearly disappear. Properly protected rain water will then contain less life than spring water. In some places where rain water is much used for drinking, this process is called "curing," and rain water is not considered fit to drink until it is "cured." Owing to the bacterial life, or perhaps bacterial death, rain water smells unpleasantly from a day or two after its fall, until this curing is complete. Boiling does away with the smell and the life or death that makes it. The water of a district is an important matter of investigation from the point of view of its mineral contents. It is still more so in regard to the life it may contain. Water permits the life of a large number of bacteria inimical to man, such as those of malaria, typhoid fever, etc. Malarial districts invariably have

12

their waters charged with malarial bacteria. Boiling the water destroys all bacterial life although not always the germs. Freezing does not produce this result, for a great variety of living bacteria and germs have been found in ice.

The temperature at which water is used is an element in its effects upon the constitution. Hot water in the stomach has a contracting effect, and if persisted in probably weakens the digestion. It is, for its contracting effect, good in catarrh of the stomach, and in some other troubles. Very cold water, as ice-water, is bad, for energy must be expended to overcome its temperature before any digestion can go on. If one will hold, for five minutes, a glass of ice-water closely in the hand, they will better understand what the energy required for this is. The feeling in the hand will be disagreeable, indicating a protest of nature against the cold. The stomach cannot make this protest with any approach to the force of the hand, because it lacks the nerves of sensation to do it with. Besides this, an excessive amount of icy cold material of any kind introduced into the stomach gives a shock, proportioned to its quantity, to the solar plexus.

This is a nerve centre governing the work of the stomach. Its injury cannot but be felt by the whole system.

Well water is always liable to contamination from cess-pools, the seepage of stable yards, or from surface drainage. So also is river water, the water-shed of which contains households or settlements. Such water should be boiled before use, especially where typhoid fever, malarial maladies, or other diseases, the germs of bacteria of which may be carried in water, are prevalent.

Air is a constant necessity to man. A few cases are on record of persons surviving after being deprived of air for more than five minutes. The testimony is, however, open to question. Five minutes is a pretty certain limit for the maintenance of human life without air. To the extent that air is changed from its normal composition by germs, dust, or gases it becomes less serviceable to man. The importance of pure air is too apparent to need demonstration.

Air is a fluid composed of 20.81 parts of oxygen to 79.19 of nitrogen. The oxygen, as far as we know, is the only part used by man.

It envelopes the earth to the height of about six miles from the sea level. The oxygen diminishes in each cubic foot of air as we ascend above the sea, till at last there is insufficient to sustain life. In places below the sea, such as some mines, the foundation excavations of the Brooklyn Bridge, etc., the increased concentration of the air and its pressure causes many inconveniences, and sometimes disease.

As human beings are now constituted, there must be some standard as to the amount of oxygen contained in a cubic foot of air which is best for the life interests of man. It is certain that man can live and prosper at the sea level, and to a considerable height above it. There

is not only a limit to life, however, owing to the paucity
of oxygen due to great elevations, but also a limit at a
much less elevation to the possibility of the greatest
human development in any line.

As the oxygen to the cubic foot is diminished, the
heart and lungs are obliged to increase their work to
properly relieve and revivify the blood with the oxygen
of the air.

So, we find, the number of respirations and heart beats
in animals increase with the elevation at which they are
above the sea.

At high elevations a great deal of energy must be
diverted from other things to the heart and lungs to
produce a proper diet of air.

This cannot be permanently advantageous to man.
It may very well be that a man descended from active
ancestors, but himself leading a sedentary life, would
be better several thousand feet above the sea than at its
level. Because at the sea level his lungs, accustomed to
activity in his ancestors, would receive too little exercise
to maintain their health in his own sedentary body,
whereas at the high elevation they might exercise
as much as those of an athlete at a lower level. The
preference that disease has for unused as for overused
organs makes it seem probable, that the rapid proportionate increase in civilization of those leading sedentary lives, but descended from more active ancestors, is
an element in the increase of lung troubles. If this be
true we can understand why high elevations may be

beneficial for such subjects. Though the rule be to let a diseased member or organ rest, it would in such case be the rest or lack of exercise that caused the disease and the cause must be removed before the disease can be cured.

Air over the ocean, a few miles from the land, and also at high altitudes, is comparatively free from germs and dust. Air thus pure is better than when impure, especially for diseased lungs. This quality may overcome to a certain extent the drawbacks of lack of oxygen at high altitudes. The exemptions in the French conscription due to deficiencies of body or mind, are found to increase in a rising ratio with each thousand feet of elevation after two thousand feet above the sea. This is a clear indication that high elevations are not aids to the highest development of man.

A number of examinations of mountain populations, and of those upon elevated plateaus, leads me to advise strongly against any permanent residence over two thousand feet above the sea.

Air is much vitiated by swamps. These should not be selected as residences, nor should places near them. The efficiency and force of the individual is lowered by such air, and the rearing of a family becomes doubtful. The vitality of air is diminished by human use. Consequently the air, in cities where large numbers of human beings are congregated together, is less good than that of the country.

While a young man in business in Baltimore I was in

the habit of spending my Sunday afternoons in the country. I can recollect very well the dull, heavy feeling of the air of the city when returning in the evening. The fresh and strong feeling of the country air, when going out of the city into it, is also a vivid recollection in my mind. Closed rooms, ill-ventilated buildings, or places where many people congregate in one room as in tenement houses, theatres, etc., are all disadvantageous to the highest evolution of human energy. Frequent or long exposures to such conditions should be avoided. In certain trades and occupations a great deal of dust gets into the air breathed by the operatives. Such trades or occupations are all unhealthy, especially tending to consumption. The prudent will not engage in such occupations.

An extended series of observations by Dr. W. B. Wood has warranted him in estimating that four sevenths of the entire population are affected by lung complaints. The dissections at the Salpétrière, the great French hospital for the insane, show a still larger proportion to be or to have been affected by tubercular lesions in the lungs. Consumption is a disease of civilization. The disease, as far as I know, was never observed in any savage people when first visited by Europeans. It is still very little known amongst such peoples. Our pioneer life has had a curative effect upon consumption. Thus we see the consumptive early settlers in our Western States benefited or cured of the malady, whereas to-day in the high civilization that has followed the old primitive life we find the population of the same districts where cures were formerly the rule now rank producers of consumption. A larger proportion of the population is consumptive in New England and the coast provinces of Canada than anywhere else in the world. The standard of life in these places is high, the time and energy demanded for education great, and the strain upon the nervous system heavy. Consumption in its prevalence generally corresponds with nervous strain. A recently published sanitary atlas will show this relation. The exceptions occur where the lungs are much irritated by dust, foul air, etc. These things indicate that the opinion that phthisis is a disease due to nervous debility or nervous overstrain has some reason in it. At the same time we must admit that this disease has other causes. The bacillus tuberculosis is found in those diseased with it, and the disease may be created, in animals at least, by inoculations of this bacillus. It is also a generally received opinion that those with consumption may infect persons living with them. The disinfecting methods for the sputa, etc., lately adopted in hospitals for consumptives, as at Brompton, show a great benefit in reduced intensity of the disease, prolonged average of life, and increased proportions of cures. It is evident, then, that the bacillus plays an important part in the causation, intensity, or continuance of consumption. At the same time we must remember that the injection into the blood of certain ptomaines found in dead bodies will cause death, so also will the various bacteria that produce them. We

cannot on this account attribute death in general to
these bacteria.

But we say that death is due to a lack of force sufficient to maintain the necessary functions of one or more
of the vital organs. After death we admit that certain
bacteria are found normally in the cadaver, but we do
not admit that these were the cause of death, although
they may be made to again produce it. A paper was
recently communicated to the Academy of Sciences at
Paris, by Dr. Curmont, Preparator of the School of Medicine at Lyons, on a new bacillary tuberculosis of bovine
origin. He claims that he has found a new bacillus
capable of producing tuberculosis. His proof lies in the
fact that he has caused tuberculosis in rabbits by inocu-
lation of the new bacillus. In Guinea pigs it does not
produce tuberculosis, but it causes a general infection
which is fatal. May it not be the consumption, the diseased state, which makes the condition favorable to the
life and multiplication of the bacillus tuberculosis,
whether of the old kind or of the claimed new sort?
Consumption is certainly not a climatic disease, for it
is found present or absent in all sorts of climates. It is
common in the south of Scotland and almost unknown
in the north of Scotland. It is common throughout England although very rare in the southwest. Common in
Denmark, it is practically absent in the phenomenally
bad climate of Iceland. A scourge in New England and
Nova Scotia, it is a curiosity in the old Hudson Bay
country. Common in Central Europe it is confined to

the political prisoners in Eastern Siberia. Whatever may
be its cause it is never general except when the nervous
system is under a heavy strain. Under these conditions
it is always prevalent. As our progress is upon nervous
lines, it is apparent that consumption is a disease especially to be guarded against.

Those occupations or situations where it is to be most
expected from irritation to the lungs, confinement, etc.,
and in which no nervous progress or development is
especially at stake, should be religiously relegated to
those without an expectation of immortality in the child.

The temperature of the air is an influential factor in
the human activity. In the far north a great amount of
energy is required to assimilate the fats necessary to
maintain the heat of the body and generally to resist the
extreme cold. Very cold climates do not permit intellectual activity, on account of their absorption of energy
to resist their low temperatures. The extensions toward
the north of the line of the highest civilization, it is to
be presumed, is due to the devices of man in counteracting the cold. The most prominent of these is in the
application of artificial heat and in the housing of the
people, by both of which the energies are saved.

In the tropics the paucity of intellectual activity is still
more noticeable. For the population in the tropics is
much greater from which such manifestations could come
and of greatly longer residence. Manifestly the arctic
regions have only been inhabited by reason of population pressure from more fortunate regions. Consequently

they must have been settled last of all the corners of the earth.

Any activity of the body or brain is accompanied by heat which must be gotten rid of when it is in excess of the bodily needs. No considerable exertion can be undertaken in a hot climate without such excess of heat-production. The energies required for such heat elimination in an active person so situated are very great. Where warm climates are also humid, the difficulty of getting rid of surplus body heat is increased. Such elimination of heat in man is produced by perspiration and evaporation. The greater the humidity of the air, the temperature being equal, the slower must be the evaporation and consequent cooling of the body. From these matters we may perceive a reasonable explanation of the body and mind indolence of the world's tropical population.

Every activity under the equator requires much energy to get rid of the heat it produces, while in the cooler zones activity for the production of heat is more and more a necessity to preserve life. Cold, therefore, must be beneficial to progress, until it reaches a point where the energies are all or nearly all absorbed to counteract it. From these considerations it will be plain that every one, desiring for himself and his descendants the highest estate of man, will select the temperate or cool zone for his residence. Dry heat, being more favorable to evaporation and cooling, is less obnoxious to the evolution of human energy. We have no historical record of a high civilization in a moist, hot climate, nor does such a civilization exist, neither is it to be expected. The Mexican and Peruvian civilizations were of an inferior character, and also in high, comparatively cool altitudes, and dry districts where tropical conditions were much modified. A few ruins here and there in the tropics are found, as in Central America, Ceylon, Siam, etc. They are all of a primitive type, and as the record is a blank regarding their history, we may presume that even these are due to some emigrants not long maintaining their imported energy.

Alexander Hamilton, like a few other distinguished persons, was born in the tropics, but of parents from more favorable climes, and his activities were in the temperate zone.

Hamilton was born in the West Indies ; D'Éspréménil in Madras, and Fournier in Martinique. The Vasa family is about the only distinguished one from the far north. No distinguished person in the world's history comes from within the arctic circle, nor four degrees from the equator. This rather smooth theory has one bad stumbling-block to contend on the heat side. It is that the greatest athletic performances of men or animals have been on warm or hot days, and not on cold ones. My own experience in athletic games is that I work better on a warm or hot day, and feel my skill markedly diminished on a cold or even chilly one. Consequently, the efforts of nature to overcome the heat produced by bodily action must not be overestimated, and may not be the source of human in-

dolence in the tropics. The worthlessness of tropical
population, no matter from where recruited, makes the
tropics forbidden ground for the family founder.

A universal accompaniment of the advance of man
has been the discovery and use of some form of stimulant or narcotic. All of them, if we except the mild
cocoa, have a disagreeable first taste that must be overcome by habit or disguised by flavoring.

Children do not like the natural taste of any of these
agents. The effect of the first use of some of them, as
tobacco, are unpleasant. We class them as stimulants or
narcotics. As a matter of fact, however, they are all
narcotic when taken in sufficient quantity. On the
other hand, pronounced narcotics, even such as ether,
have a preliminary stimulating or exciting effect.

It is beyond the scope of this work to treat exhaus-
tively of all agents of this kind, therefore, a sketch will
be given only of those in most common use.

These are of so-called stimulants, tea, coffee, and alcohol, and of narcotics, tobacco and opium. In South
America *mate*, whose active principle is thein, and
coca are largely used, while in Africa it is the kola nut,
with thein or coffeine as its principle ; in India Indian
hemp, etc., but as these drugs are not much used
amongst us, we need not discuss them except to say that
the habitual use of coca has great dangers, and Indian
hemp still greater. The latter should never be used, for
the same reasons that will subsequently be given for the
total abstinence from opium.

TEA.—Tea is produced from the leaves of a plant grown principally in China and India. It owes its stimulating properties to an alkaloid known as thein, discovered by Oudry in 1827. It is properly prepared by pouring boiling-hot water on the leaves. In proportion to the time that this water is poured from the leaves the character of the beverage is influenced. The quicker it is done the more of the delicate aroma of the leaves will be had, and the less of the thein and astringent properties of the leaves. Perfect tea cannot be allowed to stand long on the leaves, and should be drunk immediately after preparation. As thus used it is a delightful drink with no known deleterious effects. This sort of tea is not often made outside of China. As usually prepared it is stronger, slightly stimulating, and little subject to abuse. When used in large quantities, however, it is apt to have an unfavorable effect upon the digestion, perhaps as much through the excess of tannin from the usually stewed leaves as from the excess of thein. Excess in the use of tea also produces a condition called nervousness, characterized by tremor in the muscles, sleeplessness, and incapacity for full body or mind work.

In the Wigan district in England the female operatives used a considerable amount of very strong tea. To such an extent was this practice carried that the health of these operatives was often ruined, and they were found to be tea drunkards. A medical inquiry into the condition of the Wigan operatives, attributed to the tea

habit the nervous break-down of the women, their hys-
teria, and the general ruin of their health. It is only in
large doses that such results are produced, but like all
the stimulants or narcotics it is subject to obtain an empire over its users, to their injury or ruin. Like all the
agents containing thein, the known effects of tea are
upon the spinal cord and upon the cerebrum, and doubtless, secondarily, more or less upon all the nervous
centres.

In moderation it probably aids mental work. At least
this is the seeming effect.

COFFEE.—Coffee is made from the berry of a bush
growing in Arabia, Ceylon, Java, Brazil, Mexico, Central America, and a few other places.

It is prepared by roasting the berry, grinding it, and
pouring boiling water upon it. Coffee is like tea, in containing thein or caffeine which was discovered in it by
Runge in 1820, and identified with thein by Mulder and
Jobst in 1838. It differs from tea in containing less
astringent and in having an empyreumatic oil which
alone has marked stimulating properties. Coffee, to be
at its best, should be made strong. It may then be adulterated with hot milk and cream without loss of flavor.
Weak tea may be excellent, but weak coffee is an abom-
ination. Coffee, perhaps for this reason, is drunk
stronger than tea, and has a marked stimulating effect
upon the nervous system. Used to excess it will produce
the same results as tea, and also others, such as neu-
ralgia and headache. It is said to be an aphrodesiac.

Coffee also affects the kidneys and bladder, causing a free secretion of urine and frequent micturition, but a diminished amount of urea. In fact this latter result is common to all these agents. With some persons who take tea without difficulty, coffee produces digestive trouble, apparently due to derangement of the functions of the liver. With the great majority of persons, coffee is more a help than a hindrance to assimilation. It probably causes much less indigestion than tea. A perfect cup of coffee is the most delicious beverage in the world. I cannot refrain from saying something that may make trouble in the kitchen. It is that a perfect cup of coffee requires that the berry should have been roasted and ground immediately before it was made. The medical officers of the French army use it as a preventative of malaria instead of quinine, and claim good results from it. Coffee reduces the heart beats while increasing the heart force. On this account it has been found useful in weak heart, and in dropsy due to heart disease. Coffee has less cumulative action than digitalis, a drug used for the same diseases, and is on this account better.

ALCOHOL.—Alcohol is a colorless volatile fluid formed out of sugar by fermentation. It is always taken diluted very much with water, and the more the better. Whiskey and brandy, amongst the strongest forms in which it is used, are generally expected to contain from 48 to 56 per cent. of alcohol. Beer and wine are the other common forms of alcohol in use in this country, both of which vary in strength, but are very much weaker than those first named. While its vehicle has some influence on its results, the general effect of alcohol is always the same. The researches of Dujardin-Beaumetz show that some kinds of alcohol are more poisonous than others. His table of the poisonous dose per kilo (2 lbs.) of body weight sufficient to kill in 24 to 36 hours of the different alcohols is as follows :

Ethyl alcohol.........	89 grammes	........concentrated.
Propylic alcohol.......2.90	"	....	"
"	"	.. ....3.75	"	........dilute.
Butylic	"	.......2.00	"	........concentrated.
"	"	.......1.85	"	........dilute.
Amylic	"	.......1.70	"	........concentrated.
"	"	.......1.50	"	........dilute.

The alcohol in general use is more poisonous the more concentrated it is. The reason that the two last are more poisonous when dilute is because they are more soluble when dilute, and, therefore, more subject to assimilation.

It has been said that alcohol is not a food, because it is recognized unchanged in the breath, perspiration, urine, etc. But this does not seem established, because no experimenter as yet has been able to find more than 16 per cent. of the alcohol administered in the excreta, and it is therefore surmised that the balance must be lost or used in the system. Alcohol diminishes cell activity, upon which bodily heat depends, and therefore lowers the temperature. It does this in another way, also, by dilation of the capillaries and determination of blood to the surface. This increases the action of the sweat glands and evaporation. The blood near the air and evaporation are both cooling. It is not surprising, therefore, to know that in large amounts, alcohol sometimes reduces the body temperature below normal from two to four degrees F.

In its more concentrated forms in general use, as brandy, whiskey, gin, and rum, alcohol when taken habitually injures the liver, causing cirrhosis. It also injures the heart and kidneys. In countries where wine and beer are the forms of alcohol mostly used liver lesions due to alcohol are not common. Its excessive use predisposes to all lung diseases. The unfavorable results of excesses in liquor are particularly pronounced in pneumonia. In this disease the alcohol habit produces more directly recognized fatal results than in any other. All muscular power is reduced by alcohol in its direct effects, consequently athletes avoid it when preparing for any feat or contest. I have observed that even a pint of claret, taken at dinner, diminished my power while in training to walk a measured three miles by several seconds. We have no means of ascertaining what its effects are on mental effort, but it is to be presumed that they are similar and disadvantageous. On the other hand, we have the opinion of many physicians that alcohol will increase the vital forces, and enable the individual to bridge over some disaster to the body which without it would cause death. Dr. W. P. Lombard has recently conducted some experiments which

13

seem to have been carefully checked. By careful meas-
urement he claims that at least temporarily muscular
power increases under alcohol and diminishes under
tobacco. His theory is that muscular fatigue is not so
much due to muscular as to nerve exhaustion of the
centres, the immediate source of the muscular stimulus.
He derived this idea from the fact that the application
of electricity to an apparently exhausted muscle immediately causes the contraction to appear in full force.
Alcohol certainly has a preliminary effect on the terminal
nerves, and the first physical record of its abuse is recognizable in these. It is exceedingly subject to abuse.
The intoxication produced by alcohol relieves man temporarily from the strain, competition, and responsibilities
of life. He escapes from society at least temporarily, or
he escapes from himself. The weaker he is the more he
is fascinated and lured on. A certain amount of indulgence still further weakens him ; his will power is lost,
his body is injured, his spirit is enslaved, and he is in
the hands of a demon from whom few escape. A man
under its influence is capable of ruining himself, his
friends, his wife, his children. Alcohol is the original
Arab name of this spirit. It means the demon. In its
abuse no name could be more appropriate. The effect
of alcohol on the nervous system in toxic doses is a progressive paralysis, commencing with the highest, or reasoning powers, and involving one centre after another,
each one lower till at last death occurs by paralysis of
the nerves producing respiration. So the first evidence

of drunkenness is the loss of reason and self control. Continual degradation in drunkenness tends more and more to make this first paralysis permanent.

The amount of crime and misery due to drunkenness is very great. No one denies it. Some individuals of bright careers have gone to the dogs through alcohol, but have recovered themselves and subsequently lived useful and respectable lives. ·We may say from these in- stances that alcohol alone is the ruin of many, as it was temporarily the ruin of those who have reformed.

The effects of alcohol in moderation upon the resist- ant powers of the body to cold, heat, and disease are still unsettled. In excess it is always injurious. As to heat, as in tropical climates, the weight of testimony seems against it, which is strange when we consider that it lowers the bodily temperature. The extra work thrown on the liver in such climates, and the tendency of alcohol to diminish the efficiency of this organ, may be the cause of its bad effects.

In the Ashantee war the English officers report that the use of liquor was injurious, and they, therefore, abolished the ration of alcohol. As to disease, its mod- erate use may be slightly unfavorable. In reports on yellow fever, especially in one on the epidemic at Pan- ama during the building of the French *fiasco*, strong ground is taken against it, but upon what appears to be partial and insufficient evidence.

A number of hospital reports show that drinkers have less prospects of recovery than the temperate. In

excess we have already seen how bad the effects of alcohol are. On the other hand, the Collective Investigation Committee of the British Medical Association,
made of total abstainers and temperate drinkers has
published a report which shows the average length of
life in the same class to be for the

Temperate	62 years.
Total abstainer	51 years.
Inebriates	52 years.

This extraordinary and almost incredible report may be
explained upon the ground that a majority of the total
abstainers are such from the necessity of a physical
weakness that has never permitted them to contract the
drinking habit.

There are people who are so disastrously affected by
any quantity of alcohol that it may be presumed to be
impossible for them to continue to take alcohol in excess.
Others of the total abstainers have been hard drinkers,
and may be presumed to have undermined their constitutions before their reform. A convocation of total
abstainers is generally, to a large extent, made up of lank
and sickly looking persons. A view only of a total
abstinence meeting without one's ears would certainly
discourage conversions. As to cold we have on the one
hand the instance of the loggers of a Canadian camp
imprisoned by snow and subjected to great privations
and cold amongst whom were hard drinkers, moderate
drinkers, and total abstainers. The total abstainers
alone escaped. The facts of this case, however, were

not in my opinion sufficiently well checked to be conclu-
sive. On the other hand, we have the testimony of
Nares, Markham, Sir L. McClintock, Alex. Gray, Dr.
Envall, Nordenskiold, and others, that in the arctic circle
total abstainers have no advantage over moderate drinkers, but rather the reverse. The result, however, may be
due to the anti-scorbutic influence of alcohol. We may
recognize this effect most clearly in the Nares expedition. On the *Alert* they had scurvy although giving out
a regular ration of lime-juice, while on the *Alliance* they
had no scurvy. In the first ship they did not serve a
regular ration of alcohol, while on the latter they brewed
their own beer and drank it. So also in the sixty-six
days' sledging journey of Nordenskiold and Palander
from Spitzbergen, while a diet productive of scurvy was
taken without lime-juice, they used spirits and did not
have the disease. We must repeat again that any favorable effects that may seem due to alcohol are so exclusively in those who use it moderately.

The abuse of alcohol is a frequent cause of mental
alienation and of suicide. Dujardin-Beaumetz shows
that the limit of safety in the habitual consumption of
alcohol is about seven and a half grains per pound of
body weight per day.

The doubtful advantage, or at least undemonstrated
benefit of alcohol in moderation, the undoubted and
demonstrated injury to the body and mind caused by its
abuse, and the misery and crime which so often springs
from its use, have built up a political party in America

and England demanding the total prohibition of the alcohol traffic. Like all parties with an intense belief, this party is intolerant, and has run into an extreme, both in its arguments, and in its remedies. Its advocates attribute so much of the poverty, misery, and crime to alcohol, that were they correct, the absence of alcohol would result in the elimination of practically all our distresses. They substantiate their position by statistics. They would show that a large number of convictions in every place where liquor is used, are due to drunkenness or crime resulting from it. Very true this is, but they omit to state that these numbers are principally due to repetitions of offences of a minor order by habitual offenders, and consequently do not represent a condition of the population. Another demonstration which they offer is, that a great majority of all criminals in prison have been more or less users of alcohol, and therefore alcohol is the cause of from 80 to 90 per cent. of all crime. They forget to state what the proportion of alcohol takers in the whole population is to the abstainers, and therefore fail to show which element furnishes the larger proportion of crime.

I once undertook an investigation of this subject. I was, however, obliged to give it up, as my means did not permit the accurate ascertainment of the proportion of abstainers to drinkers in the whole population investigated. As far as the matter went, however, the balance was heavily against liquor users in offences tried by city justices, while in offences coming up before the Superior

Judges the balance was slightly against the total abstainers. That is the large majority of the population involved in using liquor furnished more than their quota in the small offences, while the small minority of abstainers furnish more than their quota (2 per cent.) of the large offences. It may be said, that a successful criminal of all persons must be at least temperate, for drunkenness of all things is the betrayer of secrets. The criminal must be silent or he is lost. The Massachusetts labor statistics for 1881 show this still more clearly. In Suffolk County 72 per cent. of all the sentences were for drunkenness, liquor selling, and rum offences, most of them being of a minor character. Of the graver offences, 25 per cent. were committed by total abstainers. For the various licentious offences the total abstainers committed from 37 to 42 per cent.

For larceny, 29 per cent.; for breaking and entering, 37 per cent.; for forgery, 70 per cent.; for gambling, 69 per cent.; for violation of Sunday law, 58 per cent. were total abstainers. We are under the same difficulty already mentioned to ascertain the proportion which the total abstainers bear to the whole population, but it is probable that they bear more than their quota in these crimes. If we followed the logic of the prohibitionists who figure the number of those in prison who have used alcohol, and then say that the crimes of these were caused by alcohol, we should be obliged to admit also that the 25 per cent. of sentences for grave crimes in Suffolk County, committed by total abstainers, were due to total abstinence. We must admit that many crimes, and many serious ones, too, such as manslaughter and murder, are due to drink, and that there is no just reason for thinking that total abstinence encourages any crimes. An indication that the prohibitionists are extreme in their arguments is the fact that, in the interior of Turkey and Arabia, the religion of the people not only prohibits all alcohol, but the people live up to their doctrine. I have travelled extensively in these countries and can bear witness that poverty, misery, injustice, and crime are not lacking. Poverty is the rule, insecurity of property or person general, robbery and assassination frequent. Look again at China and India. Where can one find so large a proportion of misery and weakness, going down even to child murder? In these countries alcohol is, or was, very little used. When or in what annals can be seen such deliberate, cold blooded, and horrible wholesale assassination as amongst the total abstaining thugs of India? (See early reports of English rule in India.) Where has been exceeded in cold cruelty the deeds of the Arab abstainers who control the African slave trade?

With these things we cannot as reasonable men attribute all poverty, misery, or crime, nor even the majority of it to alcohol. The truth is that the criminal is a defective man. Examinations of the skulls of criminals and of their brains, almost always shows congenital defect. The same thing holds true to an extent of those who fail in life's struggle. It is these who seek in alcohol, at first perhaps a spur to keep them even in the race, and afterwards a Lethe in which to drown their responsibilities and 'their weakness. It is more the criminal and the unsuccessful who makes the drunkard, than the drunkard who makes the criminal or unsuccessful, although they dovetail together. That weakness somewhere is the cause of drunkenness we may surmise, when we find in medicine the fact that inebriety often follows strokes of paralysis, overwork, anxiety, sun-stroke, or other weakening influences.

The use of alcohol, as of all these agents, is therefore dangerous in disease, because the weakened condition caused by the disease is the door-opener and tempter to abuse.

A better policy is a rest or relief from the probable producer of one's troubles; and a temperance even stricter than that practised in health. Another indication that weakness, or the inability to meet the requirements of one's situation or surroundings, to maintain the standard of life set up in one's condition, or to hold up under the nerve strain of the society which the individual is part is the main cause of alcohol abuse, is shown in the results of the use of stimulants and narcotics upon savages.

While they remain isolated and only subject to the strain of their own dull condition, no general or ruinous abuse or excess has been observed. As soon, however, as they come in contact with a more developed condition, with a higher standard more difficult to reach and to maintain, we do find immediately a riot of ruinous excess. In the American Indians we find those least in contact with civilization are those least injured by alcohol, while those on the borders and cheek-by-jowl with the pioneer are the most injured. It will not do to say that the white man is the introducer of the knowledge of alcohol, and that it is this that has caused the excesses of the Indians, and not the pressure of the white civilization.

Mescal, one of the fiercest forms of spirit, has been known for an indefinite period to the Indians of the southwest, and without causing injurious abuse as long as no pressure was put on the Indians from our civilization.

While women are weaker than men, and consequently might be expected to use more stimulants or narcotics than men, under this theory, it must be remembered that they are not so much engaged in the outside fight as men. Neither are they so much the authors of change in condition. It appears to be the responsible ones, the inventors, creators of ideas, and the practicers of new methods who most demand extraneous aid or relief.

In the great moment of women's lives, childbirth, the use of narcotics in the shape of chloroform or ether has become almost universal amongst the highly civilized.

Under similar conditions we cannot say what the result would be as to the comparative consumption of these agents by the two sexes. We can, however, affirm that with the increased outside activity of women, has also gone an increased consumption of stimulants and narcotics.

In any investigation of this subject, we must always remember the enormously greater danger to women than to men of any abuse of drugs causing unconsciousness. Consequently, everything else being equal, women would be less likely to use them. One very serious effect of the abuse of alcohol is the injury of the body or mind, or both, of the children of inebriates. A number of studies of this question show it to be a serious matter. Weak constitution, weak mind, or weak morals, one or more of these, is almost always the unhappy inheritance of such children. Drunkenness habitually is a preliminary to extermination. In the individual it leads to impotence and sterility directly, and thus is doubly opened the black pit of eternal death. I deem it unnecessary, and therefore unwise, to go into details on this subject. It is probably sufficient to say that the proof of these statements is easy of access in the works of several physicians and alienists. Dr. Howe, Mandsley, and Morel are among the latter. To show the character of their testimony in one line, I may cite Dr. Howe's statement that out of 300 idiots 145 were the offspring of intemperate parents.

TOBACCO.—Tobacco is prepared from the leaves of a plant native to America, but now grown nearly all over the world. It is variously used in snuff, taken through the nose, chewing in the mouth, smoking in pipes, cigars, and cigarettes. Its effects are produced by an alkaloid

called nicotine. No lesions have thus far been found
in the body that could be attributed to tobacco. The
first use of tobacco generally produces nausea and col-
lapse, but the body and nerves in the great majority of
cases soon learn to tolerate its presence. In moderation it does not generally do harm, but it tends readily
to excess. When abused it causes nervousness, sleeplessness, incapacity for prolonged attention or work, and
derangement of the digestion. The effects of excess of
tobacco may so weaken the system as to lead to the
abuse of alcohol as a relief. Several educators state that
they can determine the time when a young student commences the use of tobacco. It may, they say, be recognized by a record of his recitations. The tobacco users'
capacity diminishes.

Professor Oliver, of Annapolis, says that a tobacco
using boy is incapable of drawing a straight line. Tobacco is unfavorable to the full use of the muscles, and
is in consequence forbidden, at least in quantity, by
trainers of athletes to those under their charge. Full
power of muscle and steadiness of nerve are both
diminished by tobacco. A number of literary and
military men have stated that they derived help and
force from tobacco. A number of prominent men,
from Carneades, who took hellebore when studying, to
Byron, have had this idea in reference to stimulants or
narcotics, but it is probable that they were deceived as
to any direct benefit, and that such advantage as they
derived from these agents was by the rest the paralysis

or partial paralysis of the mind these agents give, or by
the slowing of the brain activities; sometimes, perhaps,
too rapid and exhausting in geniuses. Tobacco does
not lead to action, but in its best and most desired
effects produces calm and repose. I commenced the
habitual use of tobacco at about the age of thirty, and
during a prolonged period of nervousness and insomnia.
It appeared to benefit me greatly, especially after any
necessary mental work that aggravated my troubles.
Since my recovery, however, I have frequently fallen
into an excess in tobacco, and have my old troubles return
until the excessive tobacco is cut off. As far as mind
work is concerned, tobacco diminishes my mind power,
but is a great luxury in taking off the strain of the work.
It is a difficult drug to do without when the habit in its
use is once fixed. Tobacco is a food to some animals,
or at least produces no apparent ill effects when eaten.
While in Egypt, a goat came every afternoon to the
street in front of Shepherd's Hotel and greedily ate the
cigar stumps which were thrown there in considerable
numbers.

OPIUM.—Opium is the product of the flower of
the poppy. It is the inspissated juice of the unripe
capsules of the plant. Opium is used by taking internally, by hypodermic injections, and more generally
by smoking. It does not lead to action, but deadens the
nervous system to a calm which is usually pushed to unconsciousness. Sometimes opium produces delirium,
and sometimes convulsions. The habitual use of opium

usually causes emaciation and a greenish, deadly pallor. Body and mind ruin is the result of its habitual use, which seems to be almost always in excess. Ovulation is diminished in the female, and finally arrested, and impotence produced by it in the man. It is a dangerous and damnable drug for use as a customary narcotic.

I have no hesitation in following the Chinese legislators so familiar with its effects, and in condemning all its uses as a habit. The effects of opium are produced by a number of alkaloids, the principal of which is morphia, though narcotina is a close second. The proportions of these two in opium are about as ten to six.

Opium and one of its alkaloids, morphia, are useful in medicine for various purposes, but in their employment the danger of forming the opium or morphine habit should never be lost sight of. Pigeons, ducks, and chickens are little susceptible to opium. In pigeons it is almost impossible to cause death with opium by the mouth (Mitchell). A hypodermic of morphia, however, finishes them easily.

The accurately known effects of stimulants or narcotics, used habitually in moderation, are more against them than in their favor. Used in excess, there is but the unfavorable side to present. This danger, to which every user of these agents is subject, from the accurately known point of view, completely counterindicates their use.

On the other hand there are general considerations which must make the conservative and thoughtful refrain from a prohibitory rule in regard to all such agents.

In a view of the world we find some one of these agents everywhere. Humanity has everywhere found some stimulant or narcotic, and used it in spite of a first bad taste.

In a general way we find a proportion between the activity and progressiveness of a people, and its total per capita consumption of these agents. As the activity is · large, so is the consumption of stimulants or narcotics large, not in the individual, but in the whole population. As the population is stationary and non-progressive, so is the consumption reduced. That is to say, the general proportion will hold good of the sum of these agents, although in some special one it may not. Thus in the active States of our Union we find a total per capita consumption of tea, coffee, tobacco, opium, alcohol, cocoa, coca, chloroform, ether, etc., aggregating greater than in any other portion of the world, so also in these States the daily change and progress is greater than it is any where else. At the same time there may be a greater consumption per capita in some countries of coffee, in others of tea, in others of opium, or hashheesh, or coca, or what not, but the general consumption of the agents producing stimulant and narcotic effects is greater with us than elsewhere. Opium and Indian hemp are the drugs least connected with progress. A general characteristic of enslaved or non-progressive countries is, or was, a total abstinence from stimulants or great temperance. In countries we have Turkey, Venezuela and Colombia as illustrations of this, while in races we have the fellah of Egypt, the peon of Mexico, the slaves in our old South, and the ryot of India. There seems, therefore, to be something in narcotics and stimulants that helps man in progress more than it hinders.

We may presume that it is a relief from the change and strain of progress, or that it so acts as to break the ruts of custom, and make progress more possible or prompt. We may presume any reason, but we know nothing.

The fact, however, of the general correspondence of progress and the highest estate of man, with a large use of these agents is not to be denied. As the present condition of man and his diet and life must be expected to change in progress ; as we all desire progress and hope for improvement and better things ; as no man knows what lines progress will follow ; as the past and present are the best guides to the future ; and as stimulants and narcotics appear to be and to have been a concomitant of progress, so we would be unwise to prohibit totally their use. In so doing we might handicap the people we intended to benefit, and with our prohibition of stimulants or narcotics, prohibit progress and ruin the chances of our own people in the great race of life.

These reasons make it seem wise to counsel against abuse and excess, rather than against any use whatever of these agents.

All of them are unfavorable to growth in the young. Stunting and injury seem to be the uniform effects of the stronger kinds upon the immature.

It is therefore judicious to advise against the use of any stimulant or narcotic before the age of puberty is well passed ; against alcohol or tobacco until the growth is complete, say till the twenty-fifth year ; and always against any enslavement to these agents or to any excess.

The Universe is the Will to live. So says Schopenhauer. The Force, the manifestation in movement, the Soul pervading all things, the " Will to live," this is the Universe. The Will to live *better* is a necessary result of the Will to live. When we leave the protozoa and single-cell life, we find all higher life types of cell colony organisms, incapable of long holding to a complex combination of cells in the individual. Cell combination is accompanied by death. Increasing complexities of life, and higher improvement in the individual require the inherited cell habit of organization. No evolution is conceivable without this. This cell habit, or cell experience, and the death of individual cell colonies require for holding the good and getting the better reproduction. Reproduction continues all life above the single cell, and alone makes improvement possible. Love is the manifestation of the Will to live in humanity. All kinds of love are from this force—whether altruistic for humanity, for a race, a family, a child, or sexual to produce the child, and conquer Death. Love is the soul of life. The necessities make it dominant. In its reproductive form it is an absolute essential to

both life and improvement. So indeed we find reproductive Love the crown and glory of every living thing.
It is from its power that stem and leaf transform in
color and odor to make the flower. It is from its power
that the highest characteristics of self-sacrifice, courage,
and sympathy appear in the animal. This Love caps the
climax of life. It is the beautiful, fragrant rose of
existence that induces a toleration of the thorny bush
on which it grows, indeed induces cultivation, fertiliza-
tion, and hard work to obtain it. There are stink-weeds
in nature and stink-weeds in the heart. To have one's
heart flower out in such a way may fairly be attributed
to neglect, but by no means does it justify one so
cursed in telling others that there is nothing but stink-
weed in all nature. So Schopenhauer and many more
unhappy ones seeing much, still, overgrown with weeds,
see nothing.

These philosophers lead us into no thoroughfares, and
end at last at a dead wall. Nothing, bis-nothing, three-
fold nothing ; the nothingness of nothing nothingfied,
this is where they dump our life and hope.

The pessimist leads us into a land of desolation. He
makes for the sight blossoms of ugliness, for the smell
repellant odors, for the taste bitterness and gall, for
the hearing harsh discord, and death for the touch that
is the only relief from a desert whose scrawny life lives
but to distress us.

All this is no thoroughfare, all dead wall, all aimless
all hopeless, all desert, desolation, and death.

The preceding pages are notes growing from the endeavor to find the harmonies and necessities of nature, from the search for the rose though the thorn tear us, though the weed must be killed to secure the beauty of bloom, and from the belief in a glorious evolution to a better human life.

THE END.